About the Boy

Leah Nicole Whitcomb

Starclay Publishing

For the 13-year-old girl with a dream. I hope I did it justice.

Mixtape

CHAPTER ONE

Nothing beats the energy of the first day of school. Stepping out onto the wrap around porch of my house, the morning is quiet as thick humidity hangs in the air. I sit on the porch swinging my feet. Everything about this day is new. New clothes. New bookbag and supplies. New hairstyle. I stayed up Saturday night finishing my faux locs for the upcoming school year. I opted for a green ombre and kept them kind of short because it's still summer in Mississippi, and I can't stand the way humidity glues the hair to my neck.

The gravel crunches under the wheels of Sam's burgundy Jeep when he drives up our driveway and to the garage. Although he got his license last year, he bought his truck at the beginning of summer. Now that he has his own ride, we are free to go wherever we want. He rolls the passenger window down and smiles.

"You ready?" he asks.

I hop off the porch and into the Jeep. He's wearing a fitted navy and white striped t-shirt with slightly distressed jeans.

His brown curly hair is a little frizzy, and he smells like fabric softener. Putting my seatbelt on, country music plays from the radio.

"Sam, no. Absolutely not."

He already knows what I'm about to say because we do this dance every time I ride with him. He always plays old country music or some experimental indie alternative junk that sounds like screaming banshees.

"Nai, before you start" —he puts his palm out to me speaking in his Southern drawl—"it's Hootie and the Blowfish."

"Hootie? Is that an owl?" I grab his phone from the cupholder, put in his passcode 0-4-2-0, and open his Spotify.

"No, he's classic country, *and* he's Black." He backs up, getting ready to turn out of our driveway and onto the main highway to town.

"The only Black country music I listen to is Lil Nas and Beyoncé."

I go to Chloe x Halle's *Ungodly Hour* and hit shuffle. "Don't Make It Harder on Me" plays.

"This is my *song*!" I sing.

He shakes his head in disbelief. "You're the only person I know who gets hype listening to sad music."

"It's not sad. It's romantic. We have story. Longing. Vocals," I point to each finger to emphasize my point. Hearing Halle going into her falsetto, I turn up the volume, attempting to match her falsetto with mine. I sing along with her about being torn between two boys. In my peripheral, Sam peeks from the road to glance at me singing which just pushes me into overdrive. I grab his phone and use it as a mic.

"You're such a weirdo."

I gasp and search Spotify, realizing that I had the perfect song. "Weird People" by Little Mix plays.

He throws his head back. "Not Little Mix."

"You started this," I wag my finger at him. "And this is *perfect* first-day-of-school energy."

I pump my fist in the air while Leigh-Anne, Jade, Perrie, and Jesy sing. We come to a stop at the four-way that divides the country from the city limits. We live ten minutes on the outskirts of Redbud Springs, Mississippi—a small town of about eight thousand people. For most of our lives, Sam and I have been next door neighbors. He and his mom moved into the house about fifty feet from us when we were five. There's a thin wall of trees that separates us, but since I was an outdoorsy child, I was the first one to discover the family of white people that moved in, and I made contact, waving at him, introducing myself, and inviting him to make mud pies and grass stew with me. He accepted, and we've been friends ever since.

When we pull into the school, there's a stretch limo a few cars ahead of us, filled with seniors who went all out for their last first day of school. Once Sam parks, I hop out and say, "Bye loser," before shutting the door.

"Wait, you don't want to walk in together?" he asks, getting out of the Jeep and locking the door.

"Why are you all sentimental? It's only our junior year. Senior year is when you start the 'Let's make everything count,'" I walk beside him. From across the parking lot, I hear my name and turn to see her familiar golden brown face. Her high cheekbones raise when she smiles at me. "Luna!" I run across the parking lot and into her arms.

"Naima." She squeezes me. Her accent always makes my name sound like music.

"It's been so long since I've seen you."

"Girl," she says, breaking away from our hug. "You saw me last week."

"Okay, but a week is so long," I pout.

"Oooh, you did your hair." Her fingers graze the tips of my locs. "Green. I like it."

"Thanks." I tuck a loc behind my ear and give a playful smile.

"Anyway...how have you been?" she asks, walking towards the school.

"Bien buena," I say, waiting for her response. Her dad told me to tell her that the next time we practice our Spanish and see what she says.

Her cheeks turn rosy. "Where did you learn that?"

"Aht aht. En español."

"¿Dónde eso aprendiste?"

"No estoy diciendo nada," I wink at her.

"Naima!" She playfully swats at me.

Sam walks up to us. "What's going on?"

"Naima's learned how to catcall from *somebody*," Luna explains. "She won't say."

"Jurado de...secrecy?" My vocabulary isn't the best. Neither is my conjugation.

"Es, 'Estado bajo juramento de secreto' *pero* ¿por quién?"

Sam wears his confusion on his face. He's not cultured like me and Luna so he has no idea what we're saying. The bell rings which is the perfect distraction from Luna trying to make me reveal my source.

We walk to the gym and listen to the principal give the same orientation speech we've listened to since freshman year. Take school seriously. These four years are the best and most important years of your life. Blah blah blah. I take school pretty seriously. I love learning, and school would be perfect if it was only about learning, but it's also about socializing and being a person. My least favorite parts. At least I have Sam and Luna.

After orientation, the three of us walk to our homerooms. Luna and I have homeroom together: Luna Rosalba Hernandez-Sanchez and Naima Grace Jones. Samuel Jackson Taylor branches off from us and goes his separate way.

"See you at lunch!" We yell at him before going into the classroom.

Our homeroom teacher, Mrs. Caldwell gives us another lecture about state tests and expectations for the year. I drone her out so Luna and I can split a pair of wireless earbuds and sneak watch TikToks in the back of the room. We muffle our laughs scrolling through her For You page. Her algorithm has her tuned into skits of Hispanic people working customer service or pretending to be Karens.

When the bell rings for first period, we part ways. Because I went the AP route, I don't have any classes with Luna or Sam this year. My morning classes are pretty uneventful. The teachers give us our syllabi and go over the plan for the school year. When it's time for lunch, I spot Luna, and we stand in line to get our food. We pick our usual table at the edge of the cafeteria near the double doors that lead to the parking lot.

"Hey y'all," Sam says, holding his tray in his hand. "I'm eating with the boys today."

"So you hate us?" I ask him, giving him my most serious face.

"Nai, don't start." He rolls his eyes.

"No. Go be with your boys. Your *whores*!" I whisper-yell the last part to his back and a few other students turn to look at me.

"*Naima*!" He shoots me a look with squinted eyes. He only uses my full name when he's serious about something, and I seriously embarrassed him. I grin victoriously watching him turn and walk over to his other friends' table.

"Naima, mira," Luna nudges and points to a boy I've never seen before walking into the lunch line. He's looking around, probably wondering where he's gonna sit. "That's the new kid.

He's in my pre-calculus class," she whispers.

The new kid is about five-eight with amber colored skin. He has hooded eyes, a broad nose, and bow-shaped lips. His hair is tightly coiled with a temple fade, and he's wearing a cream sweater even though the temperature is projected to be in the nineties today.

"He's kinda pretty," I say, taking a bite of my sandwich.

Luna points her head to the girls also staring in his direction. Redbud Springs is a small town where everyone knows everyone. People rarely come to Redbud Springs, but a lot of people leave. Since new students are far and few between, everyone flocks to them. I doubt this new kid would be any different.

"His name is Kamron. He's from California," Luna whispers like this boy from across the cafeteria can hear us.

"Do you think he knows Snoop Dogg?" I shift from looking at this guy to looking at Luna. "Did you know Snoop Dogg's grandma lives in McComb, and he comes back to see her?"

"I only know every time you tell me," she says in a slightly annoyed voice.

"It's a *fun* fact," I say defensively.

Luna, still monitoring the new kid, widens her eyes. I turn to look, and Kennedy is walking towards him. Kennedy is the most popular girl in school. Every year she's voted for both class maid and student body representative. Today, she's wearing a 1B thirty inch body wave lace front wig, a beige bodycon dress with a black oversized coat, and black sneakers. She's also my cousin.

"Kennedy's found her next victim," Luna laughs.

I smirk at Luna's joke. Before the pandemic, Kennedy and I were best friends. Now she barely acknowledges that I exist. So much has changed in a few short years.

The bell rings. I head to my next class, scoping out a table in the front and near the floor-to-ceiling window. Since it's AP Biology, there's only nine students that have signed up. We had to meet at the end of last year so Mrs. Truss could go over expectations, and if any of us weren't up for the challenge, it was our chance to drop out and take an easier class. Although I was the only junior and only Black person that signed up, I was determined to prove that I belonged in this class. I completed our summer assignments and turned them in a month early. My dream is to be a biochemist and work in a research lab. Not for any sappy reason like I'm trying to save the world, but because lab work is fun, and I can get paid a lot of money.

Seconds before the bell rings, the new kid walks in the class. He looks around the classroom before deciding to sit at an empty table closer to the back. I think he might be lost, but maybe someone else will tell him so I open my textbook to Chapter Five and wait for class to start.

"Good afternoon class," Mrs. Truss starts with her pro-nounced drawl. She's a petite thin lady with a blonde bob. "I got everyone's summer assignments for Chapters One through Four. I'm so excited that y'all stayed with us over the summer. Usually, I have a couple of drop outs, but it seems like y'all are in it for the long haul. I'd like to introduce y'all to our new student Kamron Barksdale. He's a junior who just moved from California, and we're so excited he's gonna be joining us."

We all turn to look at Kamron. He gives a small smirk and waves.

Correction: There's now ten students in AP Biology, and I'm one of *two* Black juniors.

—ell—

Sam finds me after school, and we get in his Jeep to go home. He tells me all about his first day and how excited he is that his best friends Darius and Marcus are in almost all of his classes. I nod along watching the town pass by outside my window. My classes are as expected. Besides the three AP classes I signed up for, my load this year is pretty light.

"Did you see we have a new kid?" he asks, knocking me out of my trance.

"Yeah. He's in my AP Bio class."

"So he's a nerd like you?" He teases.

"Shut up!" I swat at him. "I'm *not* a nerd. I'm a cool kid."

"I don't know." He grins. "Only nerds say stuff like that."

We turn off the main highway of town and onto the county road leading to our houses. Sam's indie rock music fills the car, and I absentmindedly tap my foot to it. When I hear mumbling in Sam's voice, I say, "Hmm?"

"I said did you want to come over or you want me to drop you off?" He stares at the road ahead. We're passing the big bend in the road that means we're about three minutes from the house.

"I'll come over, *but*," I raise my finger, "you have to eat dinner with us."

"I was gonna do that anyway. You afraid of Ms. Shunda?"

"You know how she is. 'Naima,'"—I raise my voice to imitate Mom—"'Are we gonna have a good school year this year?' Ugh." I slump in the car seat. "At least when you're there she's like 'Sam is a perfect child who never does anything wrong' and it deflects from me."

"Nai, my mom *wishes* I had your grades."

"Okay, and my mom wishes I was normal like you. Maybe we should switch."

He chuckles as he turns into his driveway, parks, and we grab our bookbags to head into the house. Sam lays on his bed and scrolls through social media. I pull out my homework to work on it at his desk. I finish everything except for my reading for English class which I'll do later in my room. I walk over to his bed, and Sam scoots over to make room for me to lie beside him.

"I'm thinking of doing this." Sam shows me a TikTok of the latest viral dance. "You think I can learn that tonight?"

I shrug. In the two years he's been posting, Sam has amassed a TikTok following of almost two million people. He posts skits, dance moves, and some lifestyle videos. Apparently it's good enough for almost two million people to want to be continuously updated and for companies to throw cash at him to promote their products. Although he's not eighteen yet, I don't ask too many questions in case what he's doing is illegal.

I look at the time on his phone, and it's almost 4:30. "Mom should be home now if you want to walk over."

Between our houses is a wall of trees so thin that we can see when the other is home. When I see Mom's blue Chevy Equinox, I look at Sam and sigh. Here we go.

We walk through the back door while Mom is still unpacking from her day at work. Her Sisterlocks cover her light brown face as she gathers her things. Markese is in his room upstairs powering up his PlayStation. Mom looks up from her bag, and her eyes light up when she sees Sam. She rushes to him with her arms out and squeezes him. "Sam! How is it I haven't seen you all summer?"

"I was here...wasn't I?" He looks to me for confirmation, but I shrug because I don't remember. Usually, I escape to Sam's house.

Mom takes a step back to study him. "You're getting taller and taller every time I see you. Are you taller than me now?"

"I think so," he beams. Sam is 5'11, but he lies and tells everyone he's six feet tall.

Mom is 5'10. Although Markese is only eleven, we're both 5'8. Our dad was 6'1, so soon Markese will be taller than me, and I'll be the shorty in the family.

"Anyway, Mom, how was school today?" I ask. She's a sixth grade science teacher. When I had her as a teacher and had the highest grade in her class, the other kids claimed it was nepotism. Markese lucked out by not having her for science this year.

"It was fine. It was syllabus day and having to put names to faces, you know?" She turns her attention back to Sam. "Are you playing any sports this year? Football maybe?" She elbows his sides.

Sam scratches his neck. "No ma'am. You know Mom is worried about CTE. I'm just gonna play baseball again. Maybe soccer."

"Soccer also has a high risk of CTE," I chime in.

Sam considers this before saying, "Maybe basketball."

"I don't think you're tall enough for that."

He squints at me, and I grin.

"Just baseball, then."

Mom twists her lips, and her smile fades, "Okay. I have to work some of the football games this year. I would've loved to have someone to cheer for."

I give Sam the look like *See you're the perfect child Mom wants*. He shakes his head to dismiss my telepathic message.

"Are you staying for dinner?" she asks him.

"I can if that's okay. Mom's working late."

"Perfect." Her smile returns. "Give me about an hour." She returns to her bag and unpacks her materials from school before she remembers that I exist. "Naima, how was *your* first day?"

"It was good. I've done almost all of my homework. Just got some reading left."

She looks up from her bag and sighs, "Are we gonna have a good school year?"

I turn to Sam like *I told you so*. "Of course we are," I say through a strained smile.

CHAPTER TWO

At the front of class, Mrs. Truss lectures about cell structure and function. It's baby stuff that we learned last year in Advanced Biology. I gaze at my textbook that's opened to unit 2 then stare out the floor-to-ceiling window beside my table. The classroom is on the front side of the school that looks out onto a sparsely populated forest and then the four lane highway. I count how many cars go by. There's one a minute unless the red light by the school turns green and then about six go at one time. A cardinal teeters around the bushes by the base of the window. I wonder what it's looking for.

As I'm looking at the bird, I hear sounds that sound vaguely familiar. I glance back at Mrs. Truss who's staring at me.

"Naima, perhaps, you can help us with this question."

I gulp.

"Why do plants need both chloroplasts and mitochondria?"

I twist my fingers under my desk trying to concentrate. Chloroplasts make chlorophyll which is used to make food for the plants. Mitochondria is the powerhouse of the cell.

It makes energy. So maybe, "Mitochondria makes the energy that other organelles like chloroplast use to make food."

She twists her lips and then sighs. "You're on the right track, but that's not quite the answer I'm looking for. Anyone else?" She checks the room for someone else to respond. I look down at my table because I can't believe she caught me off guard. I was supposed to be better than this. "Yes. Kamron?"

"I think Naima was right about chloroplasts making food and mitochondria making energy, but they work together. To make food, chloroplasts release oxygen, and the mitochondria uses that oxygen to make energy for the chloroplast to make food. It's a cycle."

It's the first time I hear Kamron speak. Even though he speaks in a slight staccato, each word is clear and strong, amplifying the feeling that I'm wrong and good at nothing.

"That's what I'm looking for! Everything works together." She turns her attention back to me. "Get your head out of la la land, Naima."

I exhale through my nose and then nod. My ears burn, and my eyes sting. It's the third day of school, and I'm already messing up.

After school I walk home with Luna instead of going to my house with Sam. The birds chirping in the trees act as our soundtrack. My focus is on my feet dragging across the pavement while I ruminate on missing that question in fifth period. Luna is too glued to her phone to notice my dismay, and I'm grateful.

Luna lives in town—not far from the high school—in a red brick house. Her father sits on the couch watching ESPN when we walk in. Seeing us, he jumps up from his seat. "Naima, I didn't know you were coming today."

"Yeah, we wanted to get ready for homecoming," I explain. Although it's two months away, the school released this year's theme, and we wanted to make sure we have enough time to plan and coordinate our outfits. "Hope that's okay."

"Of course it's okay."

When Luna walks to the kitchen, Mr. Hernandez stands next to me, puts his hand on my shoulder and whispers in his gruff accent, "Did you do it?"

"Yes," I whisper back.

"What did she do?"

"She was like, 'Oh my God. Who taught you that?'"

I wave my arms around to signal how frazzled she was. He muffles his laughter through his teeth and clears his throat. "Um, Naima," he speaks loudly so Luna won't get suspicious. "Hambrienta? We're having tacos tonight."

"Yeah, tacos are great," I say aloud, following his lead, while he snickers.

Luna walks back into the living room with two glasses of horchata. We try to knock the laughter off of our faces but fail miserably.

"Dad, stop harassing Naima." She hands me one of the

cups.

Mr. Hernandez pats me on the back, and I follow Luna to her room. Their solid black cat, Nellie, is curled into a ball in her cat bed. When she sees me, she gets up, meows, stretches, then walks towards me. Luna got Nellie as a kitty at the start of the pandemic. I put the cup down on Luna's nightstand to pick her up. She meows incessantly so I tuck her head in my neck and use my chin to rub her baby head. She nuzzles me back and purrs.

"Hola, gatita. Tú eres perfecta," I tell her while cradling her like a baby. "Y bonita y genial en todo y te amo." I kiss her tiny head.

"Girl, do you have to do that every time you come over?" Luna asks.

"If I don't, she's going to think that I hate her, and I don't hate her, porque she's a perfect baby. Una angelita perfecta."

I put my nose to Nellie's, and she sniffs me. Petting Nellie's silky fur helps me process what happened today in AP Bio. I know it was just one question that I missed, but if I can't fully answer a question in this baby biology class, how am I ever gonna get a degree in biochem? I exhale a bit harder than I mean to.

"Everything alright?" Luna asks. Her gaze is on her phone when I look at her.

"I—" I sigh, wondering if this is a big enough issue for anyone else to care about. "I missed a question in class today."

"Oh." She looks up from her phone. "I'm sure it's not that bad."

"I don't know," I say, waving my hands around trying to get a handle on the wave of insecurity crashing against my chest. "If I can't pass this class, I can't get a jumpstart on my biochem career, and if I can't do that I'll be a bum, and everything in my life that I've worked so hard for won't matter."

"Girl, it's one question."

"Yeah, it starts that way, but what if I miss multiple questions on the test? What if I fail this class? What if biology isn't for me?"

She shakes her head. "I love you, okay? But I think you're overreacting."

"Maybe you're underreacting," I throw my head back, exasperated. "The things we do now determine the rest of our lives. If we make one mistake, everything's ruined. If I can't course correct this, where will I be in five years? Or ten?"

She takes my free hand and squeezes it. "Breathe, girl." She takes a slow breath and motions for me to join her. I do, letting the air slowly fill my lungs and breathe it out. We take another breath and exhale it. During the quarantine, we were meditation buddies and would do guided meditation over an app.

"Better?"

Barely. "It's just that—what am I gonna do if I don't get into a good college?"

She tilts her head at me and gives me a knowing look. "You? Not getting into a good college?"

She smiles, and I let out a little laugh. I'm catastrophizing again.

"Fine. You're right. I'll be fine."

When I glance over at her, her face is glued to her phone again.

"Okay, now what's going on with *you*?" I ask.

"Huh?" She looks up from her phone and then slides it under her thigh. "It's nothing."

I squint at her because I know she's hiding something.

"Do you remember Bella?" she asks.

I nod. Luna worked with Isabella Branch during her summer camp job. I had only seen Bella on social media. She goes to a private school, but she's blonde with streaks of pink in her hair, and she wears heavy eyeliner and black clothes. I love her aesthetic and so did Luna because she made out with Bella several times over the summer from what she told me.

"She wants to meet up with me again." She rolls her eyes.

"What's wrong with that?" I thought she liked Bella.

"It's just" —she waves her hands around trying to find the words—"I just...Maybe Bella was a fling, you know? And I don't know how to tell her that nicely."

"Do you like her?"

"I think she's cute and a nice kisser, but I don't know." She bites her lip.

"I mean if you like her, why not meet up with her? See where it goes?"

"It's not that simple." She shifts her gaze. "Plus I started talking to a new boy. His name is Kike."

She thumbs through her phone, eventually showing a picture of a guy who took a selfie from a low angle that isn't super flattering. I grimace, and she notices. "He looks better in person."

Sure he does. She puts her phone away.

"I don't know. Kike could really be something. Do I want to waste my time with Bella?"

"I mean if you like both, why not date both?"

Luna huffs, "Yeah and be a hoe? I don't think so."

"Or"—I put my hand on hers, and Nellie shifts in my lap—"Like our Lord and Savior, Megan Thee Stallion, you could be a hottie. Hot girls can do whatever they want and *you* are the hottest of hot girls. Look at all these people who want to be with you."

She smiles and rolls her eyes. "Okay, I'm a hot girl."

"And a hot girl can date as many people as she wants," I remind her.

"Fine," she acquiesces. "But I need a date for homecoming, and I can't pick two dates."

"Homecoming is two months away." I wave away her worry. "Have fun now."

She sighs, still torn about her choices.

"What's the Homecoming theme anyway?" I ask, trying to get her mind off of it.

Luna searches on her laptop. I lift Nellie and place her at the foot of the bed so I can crawl up next to Luna and lay on her arm while she searches our school's social media.

"It says 'A Night Under the Stars.' That's perfect for you." She points at the screen which has an indigo blue graphic with silver and gold stars on it.

"The dress has got to be sparkly," I tell her. "I wish I had sparkly Crocs cause I'm not wearing heels."

"Naima, you can't wear Crocs to a dance."

"Who cares about societal expectations and beauty standards?" I pout. Crocs are comfy.

"*Naima.*" She tightens her voice to emphasize her point.

I roll my eyes. "It's a shoe. Everybody else will get over themselves."

"It's one night."

I sulk while we search for potential dresses. We settle on two different types. One is a silky shimmery number and the other has stars on the tulle lace. Thankfully, both come in plus sizes. The shipping says it'll only take two weeks so we decide to couch the dress search for now. I pick up my phone and scroll through TikTok. After getting bored, I go to Instagram where a friend request is waiting for me. I find push notifications overwhelming because it seems like I'm being pressured to respond immediately, and I can't deal with that. So all of my apps have push notifications off. My phone is notoriously on silent mode, and my accounts are private.

When I click on the notifications bar, there's a follow request from...Kamron? Why would he want to follow me? So he can make me feel stupid out of class too? I sigh. Technically, Kamron did nothing wrong. He just answered the question the way Mrs. Truss wanted, but I wish it was me. I wish I got it right. They're probably both wondering why I'm even in that class.

"Do you remember Kamron? The new kid?" I ask. "He just sent me a friend request."

Luna looks at my phone then shakes her head. "Have you seen him and Kennedy together? The devil works hard, but Kennedy works harder."

Today at school, Kennedy walked Kamron to all of his classes. They ate lunch together. When she got to our AP Bio, she glared at me like I had the nerve to be in the class that I signed up for.

"Maybe I shouldn't accept his friend request. It'll be too much drama," I say.

"It's your decision," Luna shrugs.

I wish I knew his endgame. I type in Kennedy's username and go to her account. I'm still surprised that she hasn't blocked me. Her story is active so I click on it. There's a picture of her outfit of the day and of her and her friends goofing off in class. In the last clip, her face is squished together with

Kamron's. I stare at her face and see the subtle falsies she wears, the nude lip gloss, and the piercing in her nose that looks so much like mine and my father's it aches. I don't know how long my finger is holding down on the screen, pausing the story, when Luna asks, "You okay?"

I shake my head and offer a half smile, "No. Why does she hate me?" A crack in my voice gives away how much it still hurts. It's been almost two years since Kennedy said she didn't want to be friends with me anymore. Her own cousin. I can still hear the disgust in her voice when she said it. It hurts to lose someone over something that I can't control. I had always been the same person, but now with a label attached, I was less of a person and more of a highly stigmatized *thing*. Too stigmatized to be friends with anymore.

Luna sighs. She's had to help me answer this question so many times, "I don't think she hates you. It's just—" she averts her gaze, and I know she's avoiding telling me the truth.

"It's okay," I reassure her.

"After your father died, you were sometimes...a lot. And we love you, okay? A lot was going on. We were in a pandemic, but I get that Kennedy may not have been able to handle it all. It was a lot of change in a little time."

I was a lot. I twirl the string from my pants around my fingers. I *am* a lot.

"I'm just saying," Luna continues, "Don't think the worst of Kennedy."

I look back at the smiling Kennedy and Kamron. Maybe she's not out to get me, but why is he sending me a friend request?

Chapter Three

Luna glances at her phone in her pocket and bites her lip while I chew my sloppy joe.

"What's wrong?" I ask with a mouth full of food.

"It's Bella. She wants to go out tonight."

I swallow and then answer, "Okay then. Go out with her."

Luna puts her elbows on the table and covers her face with her hands. "I don't know if I should. This is so hard."

"I think you're making it harder than it has to be." If she likes Bella, date Bella. If she likes Bella and Kike, date both.

She closes her eyes and exhales deeply, "I don't know. If I date Bella, then that really means I'm...*gay*," she whispers "gay" like it's a bad word.

"I think if you like boys and girls, that'd technically make you bisexual."

"Same difference." She holds her head in her hands. "This summer we were just fooling around, but now it's all so *real*. Like, do I even want to be gay?"

"I don't think you have a choice." I take another bite out of my sandwich.

She folds her arms on the table and breathes deeply. I can tell she wants to cry, but hasn't yet. I scan the cafeteria looking for Sam. He's the comforter in these types of situations, and I'm more of the comforted. Luna needs a bear hug, but he's kiki-ing with Marcus, Darius, and a few other boys. I wave my hands in his direction to try and get his attention, but he doesn't see me. I exhale and squeeze my hands. *I can do this*, I tell myself. Hesitantly, I pat Luna's back.

"You don't...have to be...gay?" I hope that's the right thing to say.

She lifts her head. Her cheeks are pink from squeezing them against her arms. "You're so bad at this."

I giggle. "I am, but I don't like when you feel bad."

She blinks and then averts her gaze. Even from her side, I can see her chin wobble as she says, "I'm so worried what my parents are gonna think. And the church. I don't want to get kicked out. I don't want to go to hell."

I nod. My family hasn't been to church regularly since Dad died. It sounds bad but without the constant reminder, heaven and hell are out of sight, out of mind. I kind of forget that people still believe in that.

"You're not going to hell," I tell her, moving the strands of jet black hair that's stuck to her face. "You are beautifully and wonderfully made. You're a hot girl. You're every perfect thing under the sun, and I'll beat up anyone who tells you otherwise.

Even God." I put my fists in front of my face. Her laugh is small, but it's there. "I will still love you no matter who you want to date."

She pulls her lips together into a smile. "Thank you."

I grab her hand and interlace my fingers with it. "Of course. Do you want me to walk you to class?"

"Sure." She wipes at her damp eyes.

We get up to empty our trays right before the bell rings. Locking arms, we walk to Luna's art class even though it's on the other side of the school. As she walks to her seat, I stand in the doorway, waiting. Once I see she's settled, we wave goodbye, and I power walk to AP Bio. The bell rings right as I walk past the threshold. I shuffle to my seat near the window, sit down, and try to catch my breath, letting out a large exhale.

Mrs. Truss turns her head towards me. "I get this may not be your favorite class, Naima, but the huffing and puffing isn't helpful."

I want to sigh again because I'm not trying to be rude. I'm just winded. Instead, I sigh internally, because apparently, I breathe wrong. The internal sigh is not enough, though, so I start squeezing my toes remembering Mom's forced agreement to "have a good school year."

"Yes ma'am," I smile, having to stifle another exhale.

She mirrors my strained smile. Her eyes narrow into slits, and the crow's feet deepen around her eyes. My chest tightens because I know she's wielding her authority over me, and I feel powerless. If I say something, Mom will get mad at me. If I sit here, I'll be mad at myself. I press myself into the table until I can feel the edge denting itself into my stomach. I bounce my leg and try to silence my breathing. Anxiety bubbles in my stomach and makes its way to my chest. It restricts my breath so bad that I want to cry, but I can't exhale. I can't move the way I need to. I have to sit here and be silent.

I struggle to pay attention to Mrs. Truss. While she's going on about eukaryotic cells and their functions, I turn the pages in my book to see if I can match any words in the text with ones that are coming out of her mouth. Tears sting from trying to suppress my stimming.

"Which part of the cell theory has practical uses in health care because it promotes the use of sterilization and disinfection?" she asks us.

My hand waves in the air and for the first time, it's some release of the energy building up in my body. I wave it back and forth and "ooh" for her to pick me. She calls on Dustin so I put my hand down.

"All living organisms are composed of one or more cells?" he asks, reading from the multiple choice question at the end of the section.

She shakes her head. "That's not it. Anyone else?" I wave my hand again for her to pick me. "Yes, you Kamron."

"All cells arise from pre-existing cells," he says.

She snaps and points her finger at Kamron. "Yes, perfect.

Good job, Kamron."

I glance back at him, and he has a satisfied smirk on his face. What's up with this kid? As I inhale, the knot tightens in my chest.

She searches the book for another question. "So we're all gonna work together on this one. 'Examine the differences and similarities in the structural features of animal and plant cells. Justify the claim that both animals and plants have common ancestors based on your observations.' Let's start with the differences between animal and plant cells."

"Well, plants cells have chloroplasts and a cell wall," I say.

"Raise your hand, Naima," Mrs. Truss says, clenching her jaw.

I raise my hand.

"Yes, Naima."

"Plant cells have chloroplasts and a cell wall," I say softer, acquiescing. My cheeks burn.

"They do." She draws a Venn diagram with "animal" over one circle and "plant" over the other. She writes "chloroplasts" and "cell wall" in the plant circle. As people give more and more suggestions, she puts them in the appropriate circle. "Now looking at this, how do we know that both animals and plants have common ancestors?"

I raise my hand again, but she calls on Kamron.

"There's too many similarities to deny a common ancestor."

"Good point. Anything else?" she asks.

I wave my hand wildly and look around the room. No one else's is raised.

"Naima," she sighs.

"They're both eukaryotes. So that obviously shows they have a common ancestor because they're so different from prokaryotes. And not only do they have the same parts, but they work the same. Like the mitochondria and nucleus work the same way in both cells."

"And they reproduce the same," Kamron chimes in. "Like meiosis and mitosis."

"Well we haven't gotten there yet, but thank you for your input, Kamron."

Wait, so Kamron interrupts the class and is thanked, but I do it and am scolded? I glare back at him, but he's facing the teacher. What in the world?

"So similar function and similar form means these cells have a similar ancestor. Does anyone know why their differences exist?"

I wave my hand, and Mrs. Truss calls me. "It's the chlorophyll and photosynthesis."

"Yes, but why is it there?"

"Cyanobacteria," Kamron says. Again, why doesn't he have to raise his hand?

"Thank you, Kamron! It's the presence of an endosymbiont that helps distinguish the two."

"But animal cells have endosymbionts, too. They just don't

photosynthesize like plant cells do," I clarify, the knot tightening.

"Yeah, but the endosymbiont isn't caused by cyanobacteria in animal cells," Kamron argues.

I turn to look at Kamron. My voice rises when I say, "But they have the exact same endosymbiont: mitochondria. So, it's false to say the presence of an endosymbiont distinguishes them when they both have it. Plants have two and animals have one."

The temperature rises in my face burning my ears and cheeks while I glare at Kamron.

"Look at this Black on Black crime," Dustin snickers.

"Shut up, Dustin!" I slam my hand against the table.

"Naima! Office!" Mrs. Truss flicks her finger to the door.

Fuuuuccccckkkkk.

I gather my books and drag my feet out the door. I used to fight back, but over time I've learned it's better to just take the L than make it worse. No one would believe me anyway. I let out a huge exhale once I'm in the hallway. The walking helps release a lot of the built-up tension in my body. When I get to the office, the secretary Mrs. Dean sighs and shakes her head. "Already, Naima?"

"Don't tell my mom," I plead, plastering on a smile and sit behind her in one of the chairs outside of the principal's office.

"I have to." She tsks, shaking her head again and writing on a sticky note, probably to call Mom as soon as I go to my next class. Thankfully, it's only five minutes until then, but Mom is gonna tear into me as soon as I get home. I lean my head against the concrete wall and exhale slowly. So much for having a good school year.

Chapter Four

"It was the absolute worst," I vent to Sam in the Jeep after school. "I mean I just ran across the school. Am I not supposed to be out of breath? And she was like, 'You can't move' and I'm *bursting.* And she was going on and on about needing to raise my hand and follow these asinine rules. But when the new kid talked without raising his hand, nothing. Just me. And then fucking *Dustin* was like 'Ugh this Black on Black crime.' Like how am I not supposed to say something?"

I turn to Sam whose eyes are locked on the road.

"Are you listening to me?"

"Yeah something about Mrs. Truss being a bitch and Black on Black crime."

"You're not listening to me," I sigh and sink against the back of the seat.

"I am!" he argues.

"And you're not supposed to call women 'bitches.' It's misogyny."

"But you call me a bitch...and a whore...and a slut."

"Okay, but that's funny because girls don't call boys that. I'm being subversive. If you're doing what everyone else is doing, it's usually wrong."

I peer out the window and see that we're on the road to the junior high. Did Mom text Sam and tell him to bring me to her? Is she gonna yell at me in front of everyone? I push back harder against the seat wishing I could melt into it and hide.

"Where are we going?" I ask.

"It's Friday," Sam says. "I thought maybe you'd want to talk to your dad. Plus, it'd give you and Ms. Shunda a chance to calm down."

He's right. We both need a breather from each other. We pass by the junior high and part of me hopes Mom doesn't see us and tries to follow. I dig around in my bookbag until I find the white bandana I keep in there. I wrap it on my head and tie the bottom around my locs. Sam stops the Jeep at the back of the cemetery, feet away from Dad's gravestone.

"Thirty minutes?" he asks, and I nod.

He drives away, and I walk over to his headstone. The inscription says: *Malcolm Maurice Jones: Son. Father. Uncle. Cousin. Friend. Loved by all.* The ground is slightly damp so I use my book bag as a seat. I draw my knees into my chest and let out a long deep exhale. Closing my eyes, I breathe in the scent of recently cut grass, and breathe out. I lost Dad a couple of years ago during the first year of the pandemic. It hurts that everyone was in a rush to move on and return to normal when my world shattered. How can I move on from losing a parent, especially one who understood me so well? My father is irreplaceable.

Since loss happens in threes though, I lost my Dad, my ignorance of my neurodivergency, and my family members, like Kennedy, who couldn't handle either. It's enough loss to make anyone bitter, but thanks to my brain each memory grips me in a way that's as fresh and sharp as the original. It seems that here, in this graveyard, is the only place where I can acknowledge those losses, where it's safe to feel them all over again.

The birds chirp in a tree nearby, and I breathe in and out again to center myself.

"Hey Dad," I say and let the words sit. I wait until I can feel the warmth and certainty of his presence. It's amazing how after all these years, that's what remains, the feelings he left me with. How warm it felt to be loved by him and how certain I was that his love will last forever. That he'd last forever. Sometimes, the smell of his cologne will pop up, and I swear he's right behind me or one of his favorite songs will play when I'm out somewhere, and I remember the silly dances he made up for it and smile. It's like somewhere in the universe Dad still exists, and he reminds me that he'll always be with me.

When the warmth starts to spread through my body, I say, "The garden is looking pretty good. So far, I got a watermelon and some tomatoes. The green beans should be ready in about a month. And the corn and sweet potatoes after that." I pick at my thumbnail. "I don't know what I'm planning to grow after that."

Around six or seven, Dad planted our first garden. It took up most of the backyard and he grew everything: purple hulled peas, Lima beans, tomatoes, corn, sweet potatoes, peanuts, watermelon, berries, onions, and carrots. He even had a winter garden where he'd grow collards, turnips, and kale. I'm not quite at the stage where I can garden year round. I kinda like to set it in the spring and forget it until the food's done. Nature does a great job of taking care of the rest.

I hug my knees tighter into my chest and rock a little. "It's been a hard week at school," I admit. A tear falls from my eye, and I sniffle. I think about AP Bio and being a biochemist when I grow up.

"I want it so bad Dad, but it feels like I never do anything right. I know I'm being hard on myself, but it's just like—if I'm not excellent at all times, I fail." I wipe the tear as it falls down my cheek. "I'm a failure."

I whisper the last part because I don't want it to be true. I don't want to be a failure, but I had one job for the school year, and I already blew it. If my own Mom sees me as a failure, what else can I imagine for myself?

"I wish you could tell Mom to be nice to me." I twist my lips and peek at the headstone. He was always my defense against Mom, advocating for me when I couldn't advocate for myself. "I just know she's going to yell at me and tell me to try harder, but I'm trying so hard. I don't know what more I can do."

Pressure builds up in my chest again. My throat tightens as my eyes get wetter and wetter. Holding on to my knees, I rock back and forth to comfort myself, to prepare myself for the upcoming battle with Mom. An onslaught of tears streams down my face, and I yell. I wish this could all be easier for me.

As the tears slow, I breathe in a shaky breath, and let it go. I close my eyes—grateful for the clarity and calm in my body—and inhale and exhale slowly.

"It'll be okay," I tell myself more than I tell Dad. "Mom wants the best for me. She's hard on me because she knows the world will be harder. And I can handle it," I smile this time knowing it's true. Mom will be angry today, but she'll calm down. We'll both be fine.

"Thank you, Dad," I say.

The warmth slowly fades, but the certainty remains.

Sam pulls into the driveway, and Mom's Equinox is already parked.

"You gonna be okay?" Sam asks. He reaches for my hand and squeezes it. I squeeze back to signal that I'll be fine.

I grab my things and head to the back door. Putting my hand on the handle, I gulp, open the door, walk in, and set my bookbag on a chair at the kitchen table.

"You're late," Mom says, with her elbow on the kitchen bar. Her attention is turned towards the back door, towards me.

"I...went to go see Dad," I tell her and stare at my interlocked fingers. I'm desperate to avoid her gaze, to avoid seeing how disappointed she is in me.

"Oh," she says, surprise in her voice. "How was that?"

"Good, I think." I gnaw my inner lip.

I peek up at her, and she's using her index finger to circle the rim of her glass. "Mrs. Davis called me today."

She waits for me to explain, but what more could I say?

"You told me that you weren't gonna get in trouble this year, Naima. We're only one week in, and you're already at the principal's office," she exhales.

"It was a misunderstanding," I mumble. I make circles on the dining room rug with my toe. "I sighed and Mrs. Truss thought I was getting an attitude with her. I did what you said. I tried to control my stimming, but I just couldn't and I ended up yelling at Dustin." I reached across my belly to grab my arm and pull it closer to my body.

"I understand you're autistic, Naima, but you can still manage your symptoms. You may struggle, but that doesn't mean you can't try." There she is with her "Try harder" speech. Her voice sounds slightly inspirational, like she's giving me a pep talk. Like my autism is another hurdle for me to overcome, instead of a permanent fixture.

"Yeah," I say and look at the wall. Pictures of our family over the years hang there. In the center is Mom and Dad's wedding photo. I wonder if that woman with her relaxed hair smoothed into an intricate bun, face tight and free of wrinkles, smiling with her husband, I wonder if that woman knew that their daughter would grow to be an abomination, some *thing* that she'd constantly try to wish away and change. I wonder if given another chance, if she'd even wish so desperately for a child or if she'd be like everyone else and prefer a dead baby to an autistic one.

"Naima," she sighs. "Don't let it happen again."

I nod and walk past her to go upstairs to my room. I put my noise canceling earphones over my head, tuck myself under the layers of covers on my bed, and cry.

Chapter Five

Monday morning, I come to school prepared by bringing my fidget dodecahedron with me, and in Mrs. Truss's class, I play with it in my pocket. There are a few times that the clicking becomes loud enough for her to hear, but for the most part, she leaves me alone.

Towards the end of class, she reminds us that our labs are worth forty percent of our grade. Not only that, but we're going to be assigned partners which makes it worse. Out of all the people in the room, I'd probably only want to be paired with Brittney. She's mousey and rarely speaks which works great for me. It's basically like working by myself.

Mrs. Truss starts calling off pairs and unfortunately Brittney is paired with Dustin. There goes my shot at an easy A. There are four people left: me, Jess, Charlie, and Kamron. Surely, Mrs. Truss won't pair me with him. Anybody but him.

"Kamron," she says, writing down the names on a piece of paper. "You're paired with Naima." A smug look crosses her face, and when I glance over my shoulder, Kamron throws his fingers up at me.

Why has God forsaken me?

She pairs Jess with Charlie and then hands Charlie a stack of papers to hand around.

"We have thirteen labs this school year, and we won't be able to cover them all in class," Mrs. Truss explains. "We're going to meet tomorrow in the lab. Try to get there ten minutes early. You and your partner are expected to work on the lengthier ones outside of class. The first outside lab is due in a month. I suggest y'all get each other's phone numbers and coordinate times to meet." When no one moves, she waves her hands to signal that using our phones now is okay.

Kamron walks up to my table, stands there, and grins. "I'm excited to work with you," he says with that staccato in his voice.

"Thanks." I fake a smile. I'm not excited to work with the know-it-all that's friends with the cousin who hates me. He's just going to get in my way.

He hands his phone out to me. I see the add contact with my name in it. "Are you free anytime after school this week? We can go ahead and get started on the project."

I grab his phone and look at it. I don't want him to be my lab partner. I don't want him to have my number. I don't want him to have direct contact with me. I decide to input my email instead and hand it back to him.

Wednesdays are out for most people because they're at

church and Fridays, I'm usually in bed by eight o'clock. "How about Thursday?"

"That's fine." He grins, but the smile drops when he looks at his phone. "You didn't give me your number."

"You can email me." I gather my books in anticipation of the bell ringing.

"How about I email you my number, and you can text me, whenever?"

The bell rings, and I thank God I can sneak out of this interaction. "Just email me," I tell him and rush past him and onto my next class.

When Sam finishes recording his TikTok, he asks to go outside so he can smoke. The afternoon humidity is oppressive. Sweat almost immediately appears on my forehead and neck, but we sit on the porch as he pulls the buds out of his container, grinds it, and places it in his bong. His floppy curls hangs in his eyes so he pushes them back. The wind wafts the sweet peppery scent my way, and I sigh.

With the bong in one hand, Sam pulls his phone out with the other. The bottom of his For You Page is littered with red numbers that he never checks so the numbers never go away. I imagine it's overwhelming. My mind can't even comprehend two million people in the world who'd be so invested in some

Mississippi boy's life. Part of me is amazed that Sam can be so open with people without the fear of being bullied into hiding who he really is. I wish I could be more like that.

Sam flicks through his For You page. If the TikTok doesn't capture his attention within three seconds, he's onto the next one. Meanwhile, I will watch an entire three minute video and have a crisis about not liking it because I watched the entire three minutes, even if I didn't enjoy all of it. It's frustrating to watch TikToks with him because I want to know what's going on and he's already bored. It's the same when watching TV shows, movies, and documentaries with him.

He shows me a TikTok that I know references a video game, but I'm not sure which one.

"It's funny," he says when I don't know what's going on. He looks back at his phone, "Imagine trying to explain this to your grandkids. Do you know how many references you need to know to get it? Like you just had to be there." The video loops, and he cackles again. It's gotta be the drugs.

Sam lights the bong, inhales, and blows the smoke out. I huff a little louder so he'd ask me what's wrong, and I can vent about being paired with Kamron Barksdale.

"What's wrong, Nai?"

I thought he'd never ask. "It's just that now I have to work with Kamron, and if I don't, I get a failing grade for this class. It's so unfair."

"He seems fine to me."

"He's not. He keeps trying to one up me like he's better than me."

Sam takes another hit, shakes his head, then says, "I don't know. Do you think you're misinterpreting things? It happens."

I widen my eyes at him. How could he say such a thing? "When have I ever misinterpreted things?"

He purses his lips and squints his eyes. In the distance, a car passes on the county road. When an example comes to him, his face lights up. "Why did the chicken cross the road?"

This is easy. Why is he doing this? "To get to the other side of the road. Duh." Baby stuff.

"It's about dying."

"What? No."

I turn away from him to think about it. Why did the chicken cross the road? To get to the other side. I can clearly see the chicken dodging cars to cross a two-lane road. Maybe getting to that border that separates one side from the other and then crossing the next two-lane road to get to what I assume is a forest. How did it die when it made it to the forest? In all honesty, I never understood why it was a joke instead of a parable about accomplishing a dangerous feat against all the odds.

"To get to the other side? Like heaven?" he explains, but I still don't understand how that could be funny. "See? Sometimes you take things too seriously and misread things and people. The chicken's not *actually* crossing the road. It's a play on words."

"Okay, but who says your version is right, and mine is wrong?" I counter. "Both can be right."

Sam shrugs, "I don't know. I'm just saying maybe this guy isn't even that bad. Just give him a chance. He's trying to get a good grade like you."

Is he even listening to himself? Maybe Kamron is not that bad of a guy? We're talking about the boy who got me in trouble and is possibly dating my cousin who hates me. "You're the worst at giving advice."

He nods and hits the bong again. "That's why I tell you not to ask for my opinion." He smiles while blowing the smoke between his lips.

I shake my head and smile. "I hate you."

"I love you, too." He bumps his shoulder into mine.

Sam leans back on his arms, tilts his head to the sky, and closes his eyes, letting the weed take effect. I lay down and rest my head on his thigh, looking up at my phone. Since I have to work with Kamron, I may as well investigate who he is. I go to his Instagram and see the friend request I still haven't accepted. His profile is public so I tap on his latest post which was after he moved to Mississippi. He's in a letterman jacket, fitted jeans, and colorful sneakers. The caption is a Big K.R.I.T. lyric referencing Mississippi. It's cute but not the best line of that song which is about other's ignorance about Southerners. I roll my eyes but keep scrolling.

It's weird that he hasn't posted about Kennedy yet. I'm surprised she hasn't made him. There's pictures of him at the beach and hiking in the mountains, pictures of him with his parents, baby pictures, and him with some girl. I click on her tag and see that she's a student at UCLA. Her name is Jada, and she's his older sister. They share the same big brown eyes and broad nose, but she's thinner than him and a shade or two darker.

I keep scrolling and notice that in almost all the pictures he's alone. Did he not have friends in California?

I tap to see who he's following when Luna's text flashes across the top. Pulling the notification bar down, I see her full text.

LUNA: Bella and Kike asked me out this weekend. Help!

"Have you talked to Luna?" I ask Sam.

He glances down at me on his lap. "Not since this morning. Why?"

I decide not to bring up her bi panic from Friday. If she wanted him to know, she would've told him. "She's having dating trouble. Idk why she's asking me when I'm like the last person who knows anything about dating?"

"Is she still trying to decide between the two?"

"Yeah, I say she chooses both."

Sam rolls his eyes. He knows how much I hate choices and

believe that we should have it all if we can. "She can't have both. She has to choose."

"Um...polyamory is valid. They could be a throuple." I pull the phone to my heart and grin at the thought. Imagine, copious amounts of love.

"Yeah, polyamory is *valid*, but it's not for everyone."

I rise up from his lap to look at him as I go in to argue. "Okay, but I don't like how monogamy is the default. Say you like two people at the same time, like Luna, and those two people like you back? Why would you only date one person when you could date both? If you date one, the other would be heartbroken. Wouldn't it be better to make everyone happy in that situation? You like them. They like you. Everybody dates."

He thinks the questions over. "I don't know. It just feels...wrong. Like you're sharing somebody."

"Okay, but to say you can only love one person at a time is limiting. Think about the universe and how vast it is and how small we are. Who are we to limit something like love? We can love many people at one time, and it can be deep and fulfilling. We don't have to choose." I think of an example to show him. "Like you. You love your Mom, right?"

He nods hesitantly, afraid to see where I'm going with this.

"And you love me and Luna. And if you ever get a girlfriend, you'll probably love her, too and so you'll love all of us at one time. How can we love so many people platonically, but only one romantically?" I shake my head. "I'm telling you; it's ego that says only one person can love you romantically."

"It's cause you've never been in love before." He gazes towards the trees and the sky again. "When you love someone, it's like your heart is so full of that person, there's no room for anybody else."

"Really?" I raise an eyebrow. "And when have you been in love, Sammy?"

"I'm speaking," he shrugs, "hypothetically."

"Me too. And I still think it's ego."

He shakes his head, defeated.

NAIMA: Go out with both of them

"I'm telling her both," I announce then press send.

Chapter Six

At 12:10, I glance at the giant clock on the wall in the cafeteria and at Kamron who's kiki-ing at his table with Kennedy. We have about five minutes to make it to lab and be there ten minutes early like Mrs. Truss asked us to. I'm not gonna wait around for Kamron so I put my tray up and head to the lab. The lab is down the hall from our classroom. Each table is set up with supplies and a little over half the class is already here. I take an available table in the middle of the room and start setting up.

It's an osmosis lab so I have to measure osmosis both in a membrane and with potato cells. We're using strips of dialysis tubing to test osmosis across a membrane. There are six bottles labeled with distilled water in one and varying amounts of glucose in the other. I squirt some solution into a bag, tie the other end, weigh it, and put it in a beaker. I place the corresponding labeled bottle behind each beaker so I won't forget which solution is in which beaker. When I finish all six bags, I pour distilled water in them all and set the timer for twenty-five minutes. The directions say twenty to thirty so I choose the middle to be safe.

Kamron rushes into the room, and Mrs. Truss tells him that he's late.

"I got lost," he says, almost out of breath.

That's hard to imagine when we pass the lab everyday to go to class. He walks towards me and sits beside me. "Hey. What'd I miss?"

The bell rings for class to start, and I purse my lips, waiting for it to finish before answering.

Looking at the beakers, I explain, "I did the first part already. I just put water in a tube and after twenty five minutes, we weigh it again and see how the mass changed."

"Just water?"

"Glucose," I correct myself. He knows what I mean.

"Okay, so what do we do now?"

I exhale trying to think about the next steps. Checking the lab instructions, I paraphrase, "We have to basically do that"—I point to the beakers—"but with potatoes." I hand him the potato, knife, and cutting board for him to chop it.

"That's fair," he says, grabbing the potato. "Sorry again for being late. I had you doing all this by yourself."

I don't respond. Instead, I watch his hands as he cuts the potato. Mrs. Truss gave us russet potatoes and paring knives. Somehow the knife glides through the potato while he cuts it. Because it's a duller knife, he has to do it from both sides before it actually splits. Once it does, he takes the half and cuts it into rectangles. When he has four rectangles, he lines the knife up and tries to clean up the edges.

"I don't think you need to make them perfect," I tell him.

"You sure?" he asks.

I nod, grab the potatoes to put them on the scale, and place them in the beaker of 0.6M glucose.

"Is that all we have to do?" he asks.

"We cover the potatoes with plastic wrap and check on it tomorrow," I inform him.

He peeks at the timer for the glucose solutions in water. "We still have about seven minutes." He gazes around the room looking at the other students. Most are like us and are waiting to weigh the glucose solutions.

"So...why'd you take this class?"

Small talk. Gross.

I inhale and exhale slowly. "Um...I want to major in bio-chemistry."

He nods approvingly. "That's cool. What do you want to do with that?"

"Be a biochemist."

"No, I get that, but is there any special reason?"

"I like labs?" I really don't get what he wants me to say.

His eyebrows lift, and he nods his head. "Ooookkaayy."

"Why did...you...sign up for this class?" I ask, squeezing my fingers one at a time. Why are people always expected to talk and ask questions that we don't really want to know the answer to? Why can't we just embrace quiet time?

"I tested out of all the other science classes."

"Do you want to major in science?"

"Not really." He shrugs.

So forty percent of my grade and my entire future relies on a guy who doesn't show up on time for labs and is taking this advanced level class for funsies? I look at the timer and there's still over a minute until we have to weigh the solutions. I inhale and exhale slowly.

"So, do you play any sports or—"

"Can we focus on this?" I interrupt him. That's enough small talk for one day. I tap my pencil against the table watching the timer take its slow time getting down to zero. When it finally does, I rush to grab a bag out of the solution and put it on the scale to weigh it. I check the bottle behind it to know what solution is in the bag. Kamron starts grabbing bags out of the beakers.

"Can you not do that?" I ask him. "They're not labeled and if you take them all out, it ruins the experiment." I fake a smile to make it seem like I'm not being rude. "Thanks!"

"My bad." He drops the baggies back in the beakers. After seeing me take one out, measure it, and then check the label to see what solution it was, he copies me, and we finish tracking all the data.

When the bell rings, Mrs. Truss says, "We'll come back and

check your potatoes at the beginning of class tomorrow. Answer the lab analysis questions for homework tonight."

I hurry and grab my books to head to my next class.

"Naima?" Kamron stops me. I tap the back of my binder that I'm hugging to my chest waiting for him to finish. "When do you want to meet for our lab Thursday?"

I bite my lip trying to rush and think of a time and still make it to my next class. I need at least a couple hours after school to decompress, but by then the county library is closed. Most public places are too bright and too loud. I also don't have a car to drive there, and I'd feel bad asking Sam to chauffeur me for a project. Maybe the best option is to meet at my house. It'd be less stressful for me. The drive may be stressful for Kamron, but he'll live.

"How about five? We can meet at my house," I say, but he starts to object. "I'll email you the address!" I tack on, rushing out of class and onto my next one.

Kamron shows up two minutes before five. I'm on the porch dunking the roasted dandelion tea bag in and out of my mug. In the car, he pops a mint in his mouth, grabs his bookbag, and walks toward the house.

"I ended up passing your house," he says with his clear, strong voice. He points his thumb towards the county road and chuckles. "I almost got lost."

I kinda wish he did get lost so I wouldn't have to do this project with him.

"That happens." Technically, Google Maps doesn't know where we live so it happens a lot.

He studies my face once he walks up the stairs. The corner of his mouth lifts into a grin, and it makes me uncomfortable.

"I've been meaning to tell you, I like the green in your hair."

Surprised, I touch the tips of my locs, but then grimace. Why is he complimenting me?

"Thanks."

I turn towards the house, and he trails behind me. We walk through the back door and my textbook and notebook are on the kitchen table. I lean back to let him pass me, and his cologne wafts across my nose and thumps against the part of my skull between my eyebrows. My stomach flip flops, and I struggle to silence a gag. When he sits down, I sit on the opposite side of him, pull the tea up to my face, and breathe in the warm earthy scent to cleanse my nose. It only really works when the tea stays up near my face. As soon as I set the cup down, his cologne assaults my senses.

Kamron opens his laptop and scrolls through the assignment. He peeks around the screen at me. "Are you gonna sit closer?"

"I'm good," I fake smile and sip my tea. My stomach is queasy, and I'm afraid if I'm any closer to him, I may vomit all over him. It's not a bad idea. It would get the point across. Instead, I sigh, lean back in the chair, and put my hand on my head.

"Are you...okay?" he asks hesitantly.

I wave his question away. "I'm fine. Let's just see what we need to do."

He exhales and looks at the screen, "It says here that we're exploring the rate of photosynthesis using elodea cuttings, so we have to do one experiment together. We brainstorm another experiment and get Mrs. Truss's approval and then we do that one. Then we have to write a lab report and do a presentation."

"So what are we doing today?" I lean against the back of the chair.

"We can plan when to meet next. Are you free next Saturday?"

I can't think of anything off the top of my head so I say yes. The thumping in my head gets harder, and I close my eyes to try and pacify it. Unfortunately, Mom walks in.

"Well, hello. You're Kamron?" she asks even though she knew he was coming over. I told her several times.

"Yeah I am."

"I'm Ms. Shunda. Naima's mom." She holds her hand out to shake his.

"Nice to meet you. You have a lovely home," he says gazing at the living room and up towards the second floor and ceiling.

"Thank you." She scoots into the chair beside him, "You know, it's so nice to see another Black person in one of her classes. She's often the only little chocolate chip in there." Mom laughs, and I hang my head over the back of the chair. Why is she like this?

"You from around here?" she asks, probably picking up on the sharp, clipped way he talks. Something weird that everyone does in the South is that when you meet someone new, you tell them all about your family, so people can know who you belong to and where you're from. Mainly to see how to treat you.

"No ma'am. I'm from California, but I'm staying with my aunt, Amaya Jordan."

Mom shakes her head to show that she's not familiar with her as waves of nausea and dizziness overtake me.

"My grandparents are Sue and Reginald Jordan."

"Ms. Sue and Mr. Reggie. They used to go to Mount Zion, right? Oh Ms. Sue made that delicious banana pudding." She raises her hands and closes her eyes like she's in the midst of praising that banana pudding. Call me a bad Southerner, but banana pudding tastes so much better without the bananas. They get too squishy.

"Her banana pudding is my favorite too." He smiles, and Mom marvels over the excellent Black genius that is Kamron. My phone vibrates in my pocket so I pull it out and see my savior Luna's name on the screen.

"Hello," I walk away from them and towards the living room. Being distanced from that smell helps me breathe a little easier.

"Hey girl, you busy?"

I look back at Mom and Kamron laughing. "A little bit, but what's up?"

"So I'm thinking either Bella Friday night and Kike Saturday or Bella Saturday afternoon and Kike Saturday night."

"Different days. Definitely." I cannot imagine being double booked on a Saturday. I'd be too stressed to have a good time.

"Okay and what should I do? Maybe a movie one night and dinner the other?"

"Sounds good to me." I inhale slowly, the thumping in my brain—though dulling—is still constant.

"Okay." There's a pause on the line as she's thinking. "Wait, is Kamron there?"

"Yeah." I wrap my arm around my belly and turn towards the corner farthest from them.

"Do I need to get off? I can—"

"No. No. Ella está hablando con él."

"¿Ella? ¿Tu madre?

"Sí."

"¿Qué es él está haciendo?"

"Yo no sé. Él es me molesta."

"¿Qué paso?"

The back door slams shut. I turn around, and neither Mom

nor Kamron are there.

"Wait. He's gone, I think." As I'm walking to the back door, I hear the car start in the driveway. "Yep, he's gone." I shrug.

"Why do you think he left?"

"I don't know why. Maybe—" Then I remember that he's from California and a lot of them know Spanish. My eyes widen. "Do you think he knows Spanish?"

She gasps.

"Es posible. Naima!" she scolds.

I bury my face in my hands. "I gotta go." I slide onto the couch. I can't believe he heard me calling him annoying. I was just annoyed at the whole situation. The assignment. The cologne. Mom. And yeah, the way Mom fawned over him. I massage the tender spot between my eyebrows and breathe deeply through the pain.

Mom starts to make dinner, and I go to the bathroom to collect myself. When I use the toilet, I notice that there's blood on the tissue. Well, that explains the irritability and why I couldn't just push through the strong cologne. I finish up and sit at the kitchen bar.

"Can you get my work for school tomorrow?" I ask her.

"Why?" She looks up from the skillet that she's browning ground meat in.

I give her a look to indicate that she knows why.

She sighs. "The school year just started, Naima, and you've already gotten in trouble. Maybe you could power through tomorrow."

She turns her back to me. This was a tradition she started. The first time my period came on years ago, I got overstimulated and yelled at a teacher. We were both afraid it'd happen again so we took this precautionary measure. Plus, I was in junior high so it wasn't a good look for my mom, a junior high school teacher.

"My grades are pretty good so far," I tell her even though I've only taken one test and got an A on it. "I think I can afford to skip."

She's still turned away from me when she says, "Okay. I'll call the school tomorrow."

"Thanks." I grab my phone to text Sam that I'm staying home.

After dinner, I take a couple of ibuprofen and gas pills, shower, turn my alarm off, and go to bed. The next morning, I take another batch of pills, plug in my reusable heating pad, eat cereal, and rewatch *Hilda* on my laptop in bed. The blues, red, and yellows in the color scheme of the show soothe me, and I drift in and out of sleep. This is my favorite ritual. Fighting the expectations of others becomes so much harder when my period is thrown into the mix. I'm much more amiable when I get to take a break.

That afternoon, Sam texts me that he has my work. He knocks on the back door three times then his footsteps drag across the hardwood floor and up the stairs. "Nai?" he yells.

"It's me!"

When he opens the door, the room's lit only by the computer screen. My room stays dark, cool, and quiet. It's my own sensory oasis. He makes his way to the foot of my bed and sits down. I turn around to face him.

"I got you chicken nuggies," he says, mimicking the way I say nuggets. He hands the McDonalds bag to me, and I sip the sweet tea.

"Did you get me a Happy Meal?"

"Naima, you're too old for a Happy Meal."

"I like the toys," I defend myself. The toys shouldn't just be for children.

He huffs, "I got you a ten-piece." He pulls his bookbag off and fumbles through it, pulling out a folder and laying it on the bed. "Here's your homework."

"Thanks." I reach for the folder. "How's Luna? Did you have lunch with her?"

"Yeah, I did." He sounds a bit annoyed mainly because I ask this question every time I skip school.

"Did you have lunch with her, or did she have to sit with you and all those boys?"

"Why do you hate my friends?"

"I don't hate them," I say. "They can be loud and a bit too much. I'm guessing you made her eat with y'all."

My phone lights up from an email notification. I glance at it but don't see who it's from. Sam doesn't say anything so I know he made Luna eat with them.

"Don't do it again. I know Luna won't say anything, but she hates being the only girl at the table. And I don't like her eating alone."

"Okay," he mumbles. "How are you? Feeling better?" He rubs my leg through the cover.

I nod, and he squeezes my foot.

"Let me know if you need anything this weekend," he offers before getting up to go.

When I hear Sam downstairs, I grab my phone and pull down the notification bar to see an email from Kamron:

Hey you weren't at school today. I hope it's not me. I know I'm not your favorite person after what happened last week. I can talk to Mrs. Truss if you want a new partner.

He checked up on me? And he blames himself for me being sent to the principal's office? Regret washes over me when I realize I may have been harsher to Kamron than he deserved. I flick the phone in my hand re-reading the message. Maybe I could just suck it up for this project. I inhale deeply then press reply:

Hey Kamron,

I was feeling sick last night and woke up sick today. You don't

have to talk to Mrs. Truss. We can try again next Saturday.
   Best wishes,

Naima

I hit send, and within minutes he answers back that he's excited to try again.

CHAPTER SEVEN

By Sunday afternoon, I have enough energy to walk over to Sam's house. Ms. Tish's Honda Accord is in the driveway so I know she has the day off. I knock before I enter, and when she sees me, she squeezes me. She smells like cigarettes, but in a way that's more like it's a perfume rather than an odor. She pulls away from me and places her hands on my shoulders. She's rail thin, and her highlighted hair is in a messy bun. Her and Sam look very different. She has blue eyes, and his are hazel. She has sandy blonde straight hair, and he has dark brown curls. She's short, and he's tall. They're opposites in a lot of ways which has always made me wonder how much he looks like his dad who left them when he was little—before they even moved into this house.

"Naima, I never see you." She goes back in for another hug. "You changed your hair."

I tuck a loc behind my ear and pose. She laughs.

"I know," I say. "Every time I come over here, you're at work."

She exhales, "Walmart thinks the store won't run without me. Do you know how much overtime I've done?"

I shake my head no, but I can imagine it's a lot. I nod and try to follow her mouth as she delves into the latest Walmart drama. I hear names I don't know but nod like I do. When her tone sounds scandalous, I furrow my brow and say "hmm" to encourage her. I'm patiently waiting for Sam to come out and save me. I don't know why adults like to stop me in random places and tell me all of their business. Maybe I have a trusting face, or maybe I'm good at pretending to listen. When there's a lull in the conversation, I tell her, "I'm gonna go check on Sam."

"Oh, right. Well, it was nice catching up with you."

Catching up is typically one-sided to me. It's usually someone venting to me, but when I vent back, I'm told that I complain too much. So I learned to stop listening to other people's venting and try to excuse myself as early as possible.

Sam's laying on his bed with his phone above his head. I knock on the door, and he lifts up to turn around.

"Just me," I say.

He smiles. "Feeling better?"

"Yeah." I walk in and sit beside him on the bed. "Whatcha watching?" I lean over to look at his phone.

"TikTok."

He swipes to the next video. Watching the phone, my head feels heavy so I rest it on his shoulder and wiggle my toes.

He swipes video after video of skits and dancing. He laughs. There's a video where an astrophysicist is talking about patterns in the universe, and after five seconds, Sam skips it.

"Wait a minute." I pick his phone up and slide back up to the video.

"Nai, it's a long video," Sam whines, but I don't care.

In the video, the astrophysicist talks about how the universe follows the path of least resistance. It's why planets are spheres instead of pyramids. He hypothesizes that it's also why people adhere to archetypes about who to be instead of discovering who they are for themselves.

"Don't you think it's interesting—"

"Nai, I'm not in the mood for a lecture." He snatches the phone away from me and flips to the next video. I bite my lip then pout. I hate how when I talk, people think the worst of me. Like I'm talking down or preaching when I just want to share an interesting observation.

Wrapping my arms around his, I lay my head back on his shoulder. He continues watching videos, so I pull my phone out of my pocket. There's a missed video call from Luna. Hopefully, it's about her dates. I dance a little as I call her back.

"Hey girl," she answers. Her round honey brown face scrunches as she looks around on the screen. "Are you at Sam's?"

"Yeah."

"Hey Sam."

He throws his hand in front of the screen so she knows he's there. Nellie yells in the background so I have to tell her hey as well. I smile at Luna, anticipating what the call's about.

"How were your dates?" I'm bursting with excitement. I hope they were good. I hope she's dating two great people at the same time.

"I went to the movies with Kike, and it was good. We got ice cream after. It was fun." She nods with her lips drawn together. The loose bun on top of her head bounces.

"Okay," I drag, trying to pull the rest out of her. "And Bella?"

She exhales, "I don't think it's gonna work out with Bella."

My heart sinks. "No. What happened?"

Sam looks up from his phone and down at Luna.

"It was really bad." Her voice starts to crack. She looks away from the screen and shakes her head. "It started good. It was nice to see her again. She looked pretty, but everyone kept staring at us and...and this old white lady shook her head when she saw us holding hands. I couldn't even eat. I was just so...so—" She shakes her head again. Her eyes turn pink, and she wipes her cheek. Luna is my heart and watching her break breaks me.

"Luna," I grab her attention. She stares at the screen with wide brown eyes. Another tear slides down her cheek. "We're coming, okay?" I turn to Sam. He nods and grabs his keys off his computer desk. "We'll see you soon, okay? I love you." I wave at the screen before hanging up.

We hop in the Jeep. On the way to town I chew my bottom lip thinking about how this is all my fault. Luna said she wasn't comfortable dating Bella or being openly bisexual, but I was so excited about Luna exploring her sexuality that I forgot how mean people can be.

Where we're from, people aren't just Christian; they're evangelical Christians. Evangelical Christianity poisons. It harms. It taints the goodness of religion by taking it too far. Instead of accepting human differences, they punish us for deviating. Shame us for existing. No one deserves to feel like they're wrong for living the way they do, for liking who they like. In a religion that claims "God is love," they know so little about it.

We pull into Luna's driveway in under twenty minutes. Her mom opens the door, and we make our way to Luna's room. When Nellie sees me, she stretches and meows for me to swaddle her.

"Not now, Gatita. Lo siento," I apologize.

Luna sits up on her bed, and Sam and I sit on opposite sides of her. He pulls her into a bear hug and rubs her back. She sobs into his chest. I hold her hand in mine and rub her knuckles with my thumbs. We console her as she pours out everything inside her. When her sobs slow into a sniffle, she lifts herself from Sam's chest, and I wipe away the black hairs stuck to her face.

"Thank you guys for coming," she says with red-rimmed

eyes and a tear-streaked face. "You didn't have to."

"Yes, we did. You were hurting." I rub her arm.

"I'm just being dramatic," she sniffles, trying to dismiss her feelings.

"No, I'm sorry. I pushed you to go on a date with Bella when you said you didn't want to," I admit. "I forgot how mean people are."

"Homophobic," Sam corrects.

I lower my head to look into her eyes. "If you're not ready, that's fine. You're not a bad person," I reassure her.

"Yeah we love you either way," Sam rubs her back.

She reaches out for both of us. Sam and I sandwich her in a group hug because we love her in every way.

"I'm breaking the news to Bella in a few days," Luna tells us Monday at lunch. She stares at her tray with her lips tucked in. Surprisingly, Sam is sitting with us. "What do I even say to her?"

My lips squeeze together in a wistful smile. I hate evangelicals' ability to make people afraid of themselves. To make people retreat into themselves. I want Luna to know how beautiful and amazing and worthy she is, but I understand that we still have two years left in this shithole, and safety sometimes requires sacrifice. It's not fair, but if anyone understands the difficult decision to mask to survive, it's me. It's why I prefer people see me as weird or quirky instead of knowing I'm autistic. People tend to be nicer when they don't know.

Sam gazes up at the ceiling to think. "Maybe say, 'I liked hanging out with you Saturday, but it made me realize that I like you more as a friend.' Something like that."

My mouth gapes open. "Sammy, how did you come up with that off the top of your head?"

"Practice." He grins.

"I guess being a slut has its advantages," I tease.

He rolls his eyes. "I've only dated seven people."

"And I've dated zero. So seven's a lot."

He rolls his eyes again and turns his attention to Luna.

"Thank you, Sam," Luna cuts through our back and forth. I smile at her to hint at including me. "And Naima."

Even though I know I provided little help, I put my hands over my heart and blink dramatically. "You're welcome."

She laughs, and I count that as a win. When the bell rings, I ask if she wants me to walk her to class, but she says she's got it. I grab my books and head to AP Bio. Leaving the cafeteria, I hear my name called. When I turn around, it's Kamron jogging towards me. Before I can catch myself, my eyes widen, and I try to cover that anxiety with a smile.

"Hey," he says when he catches up to me, slightly out of breath. "I'm glad you're feeling better."

"What?" I ask, confused about what he's talking about.

"You weren't here Friday...because you were sick."

My period, yeah. I forgot.

"Thank you," I chuckle nervously and turn to walk side by side with him to class.

"So for the project—"

His voice goes in and out. I watch the ground ahead and try to focus on what he's saying, but pressure builds in my chest. I still feel bad for how I treated him Thursday. I want to apologize, but I feel like maybe I shouldn't. Maybe I'm too late to apologize. Maybe he forgot about it, and if I bring it up, he'll remember and then hate me and call *me* annoying instead. But also he wore that funky cologne that threw me off and made me want to throw up all over the place so maybe he shouldn't have done that. And he still hangs out with Kennedy who hates me so how do I know where his loyalties lie? I realize I don't hear him speaking anymore.

"What?" I say.

"What time should I come over Saturday?"

What's happening Saturday? I search my brain before I remember that it's the lab. Duh.

"Noon? Is that okay?"

"That's perfect!" He smiles. "Should I bring anything?"

"Just the supplies," I say as we walk into class. "And don't wear that cologne again." Should I have said that? But also I need him to know.

"Oh," he sounds sad. Maybe that came out a little mean?

"It was really...strong," I explain. "And I...got distracted."

He nods. "Okay, then, I'll see you Saturday. No cologne." He smiles again before he sits at his table towards the back of the room.

———ееι———

Luna texts the group chat to tell us that she told Bella she'd rather be friends than date. She's waiting on Bella's response. I'm clicking through Instagram stories when I see one about it being Virgo season. Sam's a Virgo, but the weird kind of Virgo that's born in August. I think they're weird because in tropical astrology, they're a Virgo, but in sidereal, they're Leos so their Sun is conflicted.

"Whatcha doing for your birthday?" I ask Sam. We're in our usual after school routine. I'm cross legged in his computer chair, and he's laying down on his bed. His birthday is Friday.

"I'm thinking about a party," he says, which is news to me. For his sixteenth birthday, his big plan was to get his license. He did that.

"What kind of party do you have planned?" I ask. Is it big or small? Do I have to dress up?

"I don't know." He shrugs. "I'm thinking of renting the convention center."

"You know you have to rent that months in advance. Your birthday is in two days." His lack of planning stresses me out.

Who's invited? What are the colors? Who's making the cake? What kind of activities is he planning? Who's decorating the place?

"Mom's handling everything," he chuckles. "Don't worry."

Worry is my middle name.

"Do I dress up?"

"You should look nice."

"How dressed up?"

"No ball gown."

I choke-laugh. He knows I'd try and show up as a princess if I could. "Okay, so a regular dress and...Crocs?"

"No Crocs."

"Why does everyone hate me?" I fling my head over the back of the computer chair. There's a no Crocs policy at school, too. The administration claims they aren't "real shoes" but no one cares how tight, restrictive, and uncomfortable "real shoes" are.

"Okay, I can do this," I say more to myself than him. I cover my eyes with my hands. Why does he insist on waiting til the last minute to do everything?

"Birthday Friday. Party Saturday. Birthday Friday. Party Saturday." I close my eyes and try to commit that to memory. If I don't, I'll forget it.

In the midst of my mantra, he grabs my hand. "Nai, I just want you to be there. That's all I want for my birthday."

I nod. I can do that.

F riday morning when Sam picks me up for school, I carry out a food storage container of half a dozen cupcakes. They're chocolate cupcakes with peanut butter frosting. It's his favorite flavor combo.

When I open the door, I sing a remix of Lizzo's "Birthday Girl." His confused face lets me know he doesn't get the reference.

"It's Lizzo!"

He shakes his head like *Of course* and reaches for the cupcake box. He pulls the wrapper off and slips the whole thing in his mouth. There's muffled "ummms" as he's chewing and nodding emphatically.

"I think you're supposed to take bites," I tell him. "And these were for lunch, not breakfast.

"They're good." He swallows and reaches for another.

I pull the container away from him. "You're supposed to eat a balanced breakfast."

"It's my birthday, Nai,"

"He want that cake cake cake cake cake cake," I wiggle in the seat.

"No concert. Just the cupcakes."

"Fine. One more, but the rest are for lunch." I hand him the cupcake which he greedily devours.

On the way to school, I queue every birthday song I know on Spotify so he can be in the birthday spirit. At school, Luna, Marcus, Darius, and several other people shower him in birthday praises. Each time they do, his freckled cheeks blush which I think is the cutest thing. Luna and I sit with him at lunch, and I hand the rest of the cupcakes over to him.

"Isn't this nice?" he says. "All of my friends at one table."

I'm sandwiched between Luna and Darius. Sam is sitting across from us with Marcus and some white boy whose name I keep forgetting.

"I guess." I smoosh my lips to avoid saying what I really want.

"Nai, you look uncomfortable."

Of course, I do. I'm always uncomfortable.

"I can make you comfortable, sweetheart," Darius says, tilting my chin towards him with his index finger. He smiles.

I roll my eyes and push his hands away. I turn to Sam and say, "See? This is why I don't come here." It's because of his flirtatious hooligan friends.

Sam reaches his hand across the table. When I hold his hand, he squeezes mine.

"Thank you. For sitting here and the cupcakes." He stuffs another in his mouth whole.

"Aye man, you tryna share or what?" Darius asks.

"I don't know. He already ate them all," I say.

"I ain't eat them all." He looks in the container. "Just three."

Darius, Marcus, and the other white boy are all staring at him. "Y'all can share one," Sam says and passes it to Marcus, who takes a bite, then passes it to Darius. Darius bites it and passes it to the other boy. This is seriously how diseases are spread.

"When you gone make me some cupcakes like that?" Darius asks me in a low, sultry voice.

"Never," I say, throwing my head back and cackling. Flirtatious hooligan.

CHAPTER EIGHT

I put the beige sweater dress back on the hanger and thumb through the rest of my clothes. It's getting up to ninety two degrees today. Humidity will swell. In other words, it's gonna be hotter than hell. I grab the sage milkmaid dress and try it on in the closet. When I walk out, I stand in front of the nightstand where Luna awaits on video call.

"How about this one?" I ask.

"Ooh cute. What kind of shoes?"

I nibble my lip and look around my room. "Shoes. Shoes," I sputter. The obvious answer is the white Crocs by the front door. Instead I grab the white combat boots in the closet. "Do these look okay?" I hold them up to the screen.

"Put them on. Let me see."

I sit on the bed and pull the boots over my socks. Hopping off the bed, I kick my leg up behind me so Luna can see the dress and boots together.

"I think it works," she tells me.

"Naima!" Mom calls. I glance at the screen for the time. It's a few minutes after noon. We still have about thirty minutes before we need to leave for Sam's party.

"I gotta go," I tell Luna. "See you at the party!"

I grab my purse and hurry down the stairs. When I look up, Kamron's there with Mom.

"What are you doing here?" I ask him.

"Our project?" His bookbag is hanging on one shoulder, and he pats it.

Shit. I forgot.

I close my eyes, tilt my head back, and exhale. *Project, okay? Naima, you can do this.*

"Of course." I smile nervously. I'll be a little late for Sam's party, but it'll be okay. It'll be fine. I need a good grade on this.

He looks at my dress and back to me. "Are you sure? I can come back another time?"

If I don't do it now, I'll forget again, and it won't get done. Then I won't get a good grade. I'll fail this class and ruin my entire future.

"Let's just go ahead and do it."

I text Luna that I'll be a little late to the party because I forgot Kamron was coming over, then I tuck my phone in my purse and lay the purse on the kitchen bar. I slide in a chair, and he sits beside me and pulls his laptop and the supplies out of his bookbag. When he opens the lab instructions, I try to glance at his screen, but the brightness burns my eyes. I squint and move my head back to try and adjust to the brightness. "Can you turn your screen down a little?"

He presses the smaller sun key twice, but it's still too bright.

"A little more." He presses until I say stop, and when I do, it's at half brightness. "That's a lot better." Now I can see the actual words and not just bright whiteness.

"How can you see that?"

"It says we can use any of the three designs given," I say to bypass his question. "Why don't we just do the first design and go from there?"

He agrees.

"Is there anything y'all want to eat or drink?" Mom offers.

"Can I get a Capri Sun?" I ask her.

"Yeah," she says. "You want anything Kamron? We have tea, water, Sprite, coffee?"

"I'll take a water," he says.

We turn our attention back to the screen. Kamron pulls a clip-on desk lamp, beaker, test tube, and elodea cutting out of his bookbag. Mom gives us our water and Capri sun. She hands me a lunchable as well. I dance a little when pulling the lid off the container. When I make a sandwich, I see Kamron wearing a slight grin on his face.

"You want one?" I offer.

"Nah. I used to eat those all the time...when I was eight."

"They're still as good as when you were eight," I say while chewing.

"I believe you."

I shrug. His loss. He snaps off a piece of the elodea and pokes it into the test tube. He uses his bottle of water to fill the tube and places it in the beaker. That's smart. Then, he clips the desk lamp on the side of the table and points it towards the beaker's bottom. We look at the test tube, but there are no bubbles.

I turn the computer back my way and read the PDF for real. The first time I skimmed it. "Okay, it says to add a pinch of baking soda to the water in the test tube and cut the elodea stems at an angle and use your fingers to crush the end of the stem."

I walk over to the kitchen and search the junk drawer for a pair of scissors. Then, I search the spice cabinet and pull out the carton of baking soda. I place the scissors in front of Kamron. He digs the elodea stem out and cuts it. I grab a pinch of baking soda, drop it in the test tube, and swirl it around to dissolve it. He adds the elodea back, cut side sliding down the test tube. We place the beaker back towards the light, and this time the bubbles are starting.

"Okay, how are we gonna measure it?" I ask. We need a game plan before we go in.

"Use a timer and count the bubbles?"

"What if we count differently? Whose number do we choose?"

He furrows his brow to think about the answer. "Maybe an average?"

"Okay," I agree.

He pulls his phone out of his pocket. I realize I don't have a pencil or paper and grab both from my bookbag that I left on the floor by the back door yesterday.

"Okay start," I say when I'm ready.

He starts the timer for a minute, and we count the bubbles as they float up the test tube. When the timer stops, we write our answers on the sheet of paper. Our numbers are different, as I expected.

"Maybe we need to repeat it a few times to make sure we get an accurate average." I look on the computer screen, and the directions don't specify if we need to repeat the experiment. It doesn't even say how long to count for. Who says science is known for its precision? They can't even write precise instructions.

"So about three times? Or five?" he asks.

"Let's try five. Just to be safe."

He starts the timer again, and we count. Our numbers are getting closer each time we try. After the fifth, I look back at the instructions, and it wants us to hypothesize what would change the rate of photosynthesis.

"Light, obviously," Kamron says.

"Yeah, that's obvious, but what's the not obvious answer? Plants need carbon dioxide for photosynthesis, but this one is in water: H_2O. Where is it getting the carbon from?"

I blink trying to recall baking soda's real name. It's sodium bicarbonate. The carbon is in the name. Duh.

"Okay so the elodea is using carbon and oxygen from the baking soda to do photosynthesis. So if we either take the baking soda away or replace it with something else, the rate of photosynthesis would change."

"Any ideas on what to replace it with?" he asks.

I run through the things in our cabinet that would have carbon and oxygen. Salt. No. Baking Powder. It's basically the same as baking soda. Flour seems more messy than productive. Sugar. Plants make their own.

"What about yeast?"

Kamron tilts his head to consider it, grabs the paper with our counts on it and writes down my suggestion. "Looks like we just found our variable and hypothesis."

I clap my hands. This is fun. Excitement rings in my ears, and I want to feed it some more. "What else do we have to work on?"

"We can quit here for today. Or we can start on our lab report?"

"Yeah. Let's do that."

We open a Google Doc on the computer and share it with my email so I can come back to it later. I type the numbers we took into the doc, and we search for information about elodea. It takes me a while before I realize that he's not wearing the cologne again. Maybe that's why we're getting along better today.

"Can I ask you a question?" Although I was mean to him the last time he was here, he's been nice to me today. I would dare to say we've enjoyed each other's company.

"Yeah," he says. "What's up?"

"What was it like in California? Like" —I purse my lips thinking of how to clarify my sentence— "Why would you move here?"

His eyebrows lift like my question catches him off guard.

"Um," he thinks, sitting back down in the chair. "It's not like the movies, at all. I lived nowhere near Hollywood. I can't tell you how many times someone has asked me that." He laughs, and I nod to show that I'm following along.

"I lived in Sacramento in a small neighborhood. It's pretty diverse—not like here where it's Black and white. There were Black, white, Asian, Hispanic, Polynesian, everybody. I will admit this is the most Black people I've seen in my life."

I snicker. "It's the Blackest state in the country."

"I can tell." He grins. "But um, I came here because I needed a change of scenery. A fresh start, you know?"

"Do you like being in Mississippi?" I ask, a bit worried that I'm prying too much.

"Yeah," he answers. "I would stay with my grandparents or my Aunt Amaya some summers so I knew what it's like here, but I'm not gone lie, I was a little nervous staying for the whole year. Mississippi doesn't have the best reputation, you know?"

I twist my lips together. I know. I've seen the headlines,

movies, and depictions of Mississippians. How we talk, act, and worship. How silly Black people must be to stay at the site of our enslavement. The rest of the country thinks we're a joke and often wishes we don't exist—especially during election years.

"People act like we're getting lynched on the way to school. Like because we stay in Mississippi, we deserve every bad thing that happens to us."

"Well there's a reason people left," he argues.

"And there's a reason the rest of us stayed."

We stare at each other, both carrying and honoring the weight of our ancestors' decision. For some of them, the history of this place was too painful to carry, but for others the sacrifices were too great to abandon. Someone needed to tend to the dead, but also without our ancestors' decisions neither of us would be here.

He swallows before saying, "I passed the cotton fields on the way in."

He says it like it's an indictment, a sign that Mississippi is as bad as they claim.

"Where do you think the cotton for your shirt came from?"

He tugs the hem of his shirt, looking down at it then back at me. Heat rises in my belly until frustration bubbles out of my throat and bursts out of my mouth. "Mississippi isn't perfect, but we're honest. We have to be. There are no pretenses. We can't go about life pretending like racism doesn't exist. The rest of the country won't let us forget about slavery and Jim Crow. They treat us like a landfill. Like we're the worst of this country, but we have to deal with everyone else's shit. We can't ignore it like y'all who pretend you're better than us because you're divorced from this reality. We see it everyday so we have no choice but to be honest about it. I just wish people would quit lying to themselves."

Kamron brings his fist to his mouth and nods, contemplating what I said. I feel exposed, like maybe I overshared my thoughts, but I'm so tired of people talking shit about Mississippi, and I'm not about to let this outsider do the same.

"You're right," he finally says. "I'm sorry."

I don't know what else to say so I say nothing. Kamron closes the laptop and slowly starts packing his things up. "We can um...tell Mrs. Truss about our hypothesis and then work on the lab next week."

"Yeah," I say, staring at the table and not at him while he packs up. We were finally getting along and then I just ruined it by word vomiting that outsiders, like him, are the worst. Why can't I do anything right?

"See you Monday," he says before he opens the door and leaves.

I lean back against the kitchen chair and tilt my head backwards. This was supposed to be my second chance, and I ruined it. Why am I always doing the most and not being a normal human who just keeps their mouth shut? What's wrong with me?

"Naima!" Mom yells from her room. "Where's your phone?"

I glance at the kitchen bar and see the purse. The party! Shit. I run and pull my phone out. It's 1:46, and I have eight missed calls, thirty texts, and the event reminder I put in my phone's calendar so I wouldn't forget.

"Can you take me to Sam's party?" I yell to Mom from the kitchen.

Mom shuffles out of her room and grabs her keys. My foot taps the baseboard as Mom gingerly drives into town. I bite my thumbnail while flipping through the messages asking where I am. When we pull up to the event center, the parking lot is half empty. I walk in and see balloons cover the floor. There's a huge 17 balloon in the corner near a photo booth station. Sam's standing in the opposite corner of the building with Darius.

I walk over to him and place a hand on his back. He turns around and exhales, "Naima."

My whole name. He's serious.

I grasp his arms, look him in his eyes, and say, "I'm sorry."

He yanks his arm out of my grasp. "I can't talk to you right now." His words strike my chest as his lip curls in anger. Sam turns back around like our conversation is over and resumes talking to Darius. I walk away from him and back to Mom who's talking to Ms. Tish.

"Mom, can we go?"

"One second," she says, not looking at me.

Ms. Tish glances over at me. "Naima, are you okay?"

"I'm fine," I say, but a tear betrays me and falls down my cheek.

"Can we go, Mom?" I ask again. This time pleading with my eyes hoping that she'll get how urgent this is.

She puts her arm around my shoulders. "I'll talk to you later, Tish!" she calls back as we walk out the door.

Mom doesn't say anything on the drive back to the house. I put in my earbuds and open TikTok searching for Sam's username. He uploaded a video thirty minutes ago that already has over two thousand likes. In it, he narrates his birthday party and includes cameos of Darius, Marcus, and Luna doing a TikTok challenge where they say who's most likely to do what. Everyone's laughing and dancing and the only person that's missing is me. Another tear streams down my face.

Mom's hand on my arm knocks me out of my trance. I hear her mumble something. "What?" I ask, taking the earbud out of my ear.

"You okay?" she asks.

"Yeah," I lie, but then change my mind. "It's just that Sam's mad at me and—" I can't finish my sentence without another tear choking me.

"It was his birthday, and he wanted you there to celebrate with him. He's bound to be a little upset about that," she tries to explain.

"No. I get that. I just—" I sigh deeply. "I'm a bad friend."

Mom turns into our driveway and slows down to hold my hand. "Naima, you're not. Sam's upset now, but he'll calm down."

"What if he doesn't?"

"He will. Just give him some time. Okay?"

I nod, and she turns the car off. Just give him a little time. I can do that.

CHAPTER NINE

I bring the last load of laundry up to my room to get ready for the upcoming week. As I'm folding, my phone lights up.

SAM: I can't take you to school tomorrow

I want to ask why, but we both know why. So I just text him:

NAIMA: Ok

"Mom!" I yell downstairs. "Mom?" I walk out the door, look over the handrail, and see her in the kitchen. When she sees me, I ask her, "Can you take me to school tomorrow?"

She inspects my face, like she wants to say something, but bites her tongue. "Of course."

The next morning, I have to fight Markese for the front seat. He protests to Mom but lets me have it. Instead, he sits on the backseat, puts his headphones on, and tones us out. Halfway to town, Mom tells me what I figured was on her mind the night before.

"I think it's time you learn how to drive." She keeps her gaze on the road ahead.

I look out the window and gnaw my lip. The densely packed trees blur outside into a sea of hunter green. Driving would require a lot out of me. More than I think I'm capable of. I wish Mom was more understanding, but she isn't.

"I don't think I'm ready," I tell her.

"I get that you have...limitations, but I'm just—" she exhales. "I'm worried that you're too dependent on Sam. Listen, I love him, but I think you should try to be more independent."

There's the word. Independent. The autistic needs to learn how to do everything by herself and quit being a burden to everyone else. I lean my head against the headrest.

"I understand it may take you longer," she continues, "but I'm here if you need me to teach you. We can practice after school."

"Thanks Mom." I purse my lips. "I need a little more time, though."

"That's fine, baby," Mom says. "Just let me know when you're ready."

We pull into the high school, and she drops me off. I sit outside on a bench with my legs crisscrossed until breakfast starts. Luna, like Sam, prefers getting to school right when the bell rings so I'm alone for the next thirty minutes. For breakfast, I grab a chocolate milk and a sausage gravy pizza. I sit at our lunch spot and take small slow bites out of the pizza. When the crust sticks to the roof of my mouth, I absentmindedly grab the milk to wash it down. I stare into the middle of the cafeteria. My vision blurs because it's not focused on any object in particular.

Nai, I just want you to be there. That's all I want for my birthday.

His voice spins around and around in my head. I had one job, and I failed it. And the thing is I was almost there. I was dressed. I was ready. I set a reminder. I just forgot about Kamron. Again.

"Naima, I'm glad I caught you. I wanted to—" is all I could make out before Kamron sits beside me.

"What?" I ask, trying to adjust my attention to him but failing.

"Our project? I was trying to find a time to meet again."

"I'm sorry." I'm discombobulated and tuck my head in my hands.

"Bad time?"

"My brain is like foggy," I try to explain. "I can't—"

"It's early. I get it." He grabs his tray and stands up. "I'll see you in class then?"

I nod without looking up from my pizza. The pizza grows cold and more waxy as I eat it, but I finish it, put my tray up, and sit outside again to wait for Luna. Thankfully she shows up earlier than usual and sits beside me on the bench.

"Where were you Saturday?" she asks.

"I forgot," I explain. "Kamron came over, and we were

working on the project, and I completely lost track of time."

She draws her lips together, shakes her head, and exhales. "Sam was really sad that you weren't there. He missed you."

"Yeah well he told me he hates me."

"Did he really?" Luna squints her eyes.

"He said, 'I can't talk to you right now, Naima' and then he texted me that he wasn't driving me to school anymore so he basically said he hated me."

Luna wraps her arm around my shoulder, and I lay my head on her. The tropical coconut scent from her shampoo floats from her hair. She rubs my arm to comfort me.

"He's just hurt, that's all," she says. "I'll talk to him, okay? But you have to give him a little time."

"Okay," I whisper. "Thank you."

She squeezes my arm. "Of course."

Sam manages to spend the whole day avoiding me. I see the back of his head once at lunch. After school, I ride the bus to the junior high, walk to Mom's classroom, and join Markese who's sitting in the back of the class on his phone with his legs cocked on another desk.

"Hey Bug," I say.

"What's up, Lil Dip?" he says without looking up from his phone. Bug is a nickname I picked up from our grandma

(Dad's mom) who used to call Markese her "love bug." I said he looked more like a bug bug and the name stuck. I don't know where he got the name Lil Dip or what it even means.

"Where's Mom?"

"She had to do the bus line today."

I sit down at the desk in front of him and glance at his screen. He's playing some mini game on Roblox. "So how was school today?" I ask more so to talk than to actually know.

"Fine," he grumbles. "I got a B in math."

"A B! That's good." I know math isn't his strong suit. He really struggled with multiplication during the quarantine, and over the years, it hasn't improved much.

"Yeah," he shrugs.

"I'm gonna find Mom," I say, knowing that Markese cares more about Roblox than talking to me.

When I find Mom, she's waiting on the last two buses to pick up the remaining kids. I stand near her and wait until they finish for us to go home. Once we pull in the yard, I see Sam's Jeep from across the way. He's home. I glance at my phone screen, and there's still no text from him. I sigh, go into the house, and text Luna.

NAIMA: Heard anything from Sam?

LUNA: Talked to him. Give him a few days to cool down.

A few more days? I huff and go to Sam's TikTok. He's only posted response videos to his birthday TikTok. I scroll through the comments which are full of girls and, I believe, some grown women, thirsting over him, even though it's his *seventeenth* birthday. Hundreds of the comments ask if he's dating the Latina girl, but he doesn't reply to those. Probably to make himself seem cooler than he is.

The next day, Sam sees me in the hallway, does a 180, and walks the other way. He's being a bit dramatic. It feels like I'm in time-out and am supposed to think about how my inability to keep track of time affects others. Imagine how it affects me! When I walk into AP Bio, Kamron is sitting at his table towards the back. I remember that he tried to talk to me yesterday, and I blew him off. I cringe at how spaced out I must've looked to him. Laying my books down at my table, I walk back to him.

"Hey um—" I bite my lip and point my finger toward him. *Naima, you look ridiculous. Just talk.* "You were talking about our project the other day—"

"Yeah." His face brightens. "I wanted to see when you're free to work on the next part. I talked to Mrs. Truss yesterday and she approved it."

"How about Friday?" My teeth click, and my mouth widens in an awkward kind of smile.

His smile flattens. "I'm going out with friends on Friday, but I can do Thursday."

By friends, does he mean Kennedy? I wonder if she's said anything to him. Does he know we're related? Does he know why she won't speak to me anymore? I realize he's waiting for my response while I'm spiraling.

"Thursday's fine. Four or five?"

"I'll text—email you."

"Thanks," I say and slowly back away from his table. Maybe that's the best way to communicate with Kamron. Keep it short and sweet. I almost hit the table behind me, but I turn around in time and rush off to my seat. While Mrs. Truss is lecturing, I type that Kamron's coming over Thursday after school in my phone's calendar. This time I won't forget.

Wednesday is the same. Mom takes me to school. Sam avoids me. Luna tells me to be patient. Markese plays Roblox instead of talking to me. By Thursday, tension swims throughout my body, and I have had enough of waiting in the bus line with Mom so I ask if I could walk down the street to the cemetery.

"Are you sure? I can drop you off when I'm done," Mom offers.

"It's a ten minute walk, Mom. I'll be fine," I reassure her.

When she gives me the okay, I grab the white bandana out of my bookbag and tie it around my locs. I leave my bookbag in Mom's car before walking down the road. The junior high school is right off the square, next to the county library. The houses that line the street were mostly built after the War so they are Folk Victorian with steep, gabled roofs, bay windows, and bright colors like pink, blue, and yellow. It's my favorite part of town because I feel it gives Redbud Springs character. It also helps us forget about the kind of white houses that were there before the War.

After about five minutes, I arrive at the old city cemetery. They stopped burying people here before I was born. Dad got a plot because his parents paid for it. I'm not sure where Mom will be buried when she dies, though. Huge monuments fill the front of the cemetery. Many are over a century old and dedicated to Confederates. Usually, Sam drove past this so I never got to see the names, ages, and for some, cause of death. I'm surprised how many of those surnames still float around town.

As I walk towards the back, near Dad's grave, there are fewer and fewer gravestones and more grave markers. Some so tiny, I could barely make out the granite sticking out of the grass. At Dad's grave, I lay down with my hands under my head, and my legs steepled. The wisps of clouds float in the sky.

"Hey Dad," I say. "Sam's mad at me."

I wait for the familiar warmth and certainty of my Dad to arrive. Birds twitter and jump in the branches of the tree near me. Fidgeting with my fingers, I sigh.

"I get it. I missed his birthday, but I don't know, it wasn't on purpose. He knows I forget everything. I'm not trying to be forgetful. It's just that sometimes it's so hard, you know? Like my brain is constantly go, go, go that some things fall through the cracks. And sometimes it's big things."

I shake my head. There's a mix of disappointment and frustration with myself that I couldn't remember his party. "He hasn't been this mad at me since" —I think back to the last time he gave me the silent treatment—"We were like eleven. And one summer we were playing on the Wii, and the remote accidentally flew out of my hand and hit the TV. He knows I have bad hand eye coordination, but he yelled at me." I look at the grave, like Dad's there, like he remembers what happened next. "And I came home crying and you were like, 'What's wrong?' and when I told you, you got an old TV out of the garage and gave it to Sam and saved the day." I twist my lips together as my eyes water. "He still has that TV."

But we don't have you.

I sigh, wiping the tear from my face. "I wish—I wish you could save the day again. I wish Sam wasn't mad at me." I twiddle my thumbs, glance up at the blue sky, and breathe in the thick humid air.

A car pulls up to the grave. I rise on my elbows and see Mom and Markese. She steps out of the car, "Hey baby. Everything okay?"

I nod, watching her walk towards the grave.

"It's been a while since I've been here," she says, grazing the top of the gravestone with her fingers. "Mind if I join you?"

"I'm done."

"You sure?"

"Yeah." I get up. "I'm gonna walk to the square."

"Okay. Keep your phone on you. I'll be here a while."

I pat my pocket to show her that I had my phone. I exit out of the back way of the cemetery. Unlike the other side, this one's full of trees and houses with missing roofs and windows. I pass the laundromat and bank towards the square. The square's filled with boutiques, bar and grills, and a few specialty stores with the courthouse in the center of it. They renovated the old movie theater from when Mom was a kid so now we have that. I want to walk around the square, but once I get to the ice cream store, I see Sam sitting across from a girl. I stand at the window, not sure if I should walk in or not, but when he sees me, he excuses himself, and walks out.

"What are you doing here?" he asks.

"I was just walking around and saw you," I explain. But now that I'm here, I might as well shoot my shot. I look him in the eyes and muster up all the sincerity I can, "Sam, I would *never* intentionally miss your party. I understand that you're mad at me, but can you please tell me what I can do to make it up to you? I—"

"It's fine, Naima," he cuts me off. "I know. It's that...I...I missed you." He gives a lopsided smile.

"I missed you, too."

"Come here." He pulls me into his arms, and I bury my head in his fresh laundry scent. His knuckles lightly rub my spine, and it's like all the tension in my body melts away.

"So, we're good?" I clarify.

"Yeah. We're good."

I glance inside at the blonde girl he left scrolling on her phone. "Are you on a date?"

"Yeah." He tucks his hands in his back pocket. "I should probably get back to that." He opens the door to go back inside. "See you tomorrow?"

I nod and watch him return to his date. The girl puts down her phone and laughs at some corny joke he probably had loaded. I shake my head in disbelief that someone would want to date him. My phone vibrates, reminding me to meet with Kamron tonight, and I walk back towards Mom and Markese so we can go home.

Chapter Ten

Wiggling my toes, my brain buzzes with excitement. Sam's not mad at me anymore. Sam's my friend again. I'm gonna see him and hold him, and everything's right in the world. The excitement shifts from my toes up to my bouncing leg. Before long, I'm pacing behind Kamron's chair while he's setting up for the lab.

"Are you okay?" he asks. His strong voice cuts through the air.

"Yeah, I'm good." I tap the tips of my fingers together and bounce with every step.

"Are you sure? You look...stressed."

Stressed?

I shake my head and lean over the table to look at him. "Do you ever feel like your brain's like"—I gesture with my hands to form a ball—"Like a ball of yarn and it's tangled, and sometimes you gotta move around to help untangle it so you can use it?"

The confusion he wears shows me that he doesn't understand.

"Of course you don't." I sigh trying to think of another way to tell him what I meant. "It's a stim...a stimulatory movement to help process big emotions because emotions are...somatic for me."

"I'm lost. Sorry." He shakes his head.

"I'm autistic." I bite my bottom lip and slide into the chair next to him.

"Oh." His eyes widen, and he nods trying to process what I said. "That's...cool."

"Cool?" I ask him. Usually I get a *Weird* or a *That explains it* but cool?

"Yeah, I—" He gazes at me, measuring his words. "I...didn't think—"

"You're used to white boys being autistic," I finish his thought.

"Yeah," he admits.

"I get it," I sigh. "But logically, if something presents in one population, it's bound to be present in others. So it doesn't make sense for only white boys to be autistic. Autism has to be present in all demographics, but racism." I shake my head hoping he'd get the rest.

He nods with understanding. "You're...not...how I imagined an autistic person would be."

I flinch. Autism is characterized by how annoying we are to non-autistic people. Severity or the binary spectrum we're often put on of autistic to not autistic isn't really an accurate way of viewing autism. I'm not less autistic than someone who's fully non-verbal or who has an intellectual disability, rather being verbal is a spectrum. Autism is a collection of traits that affect people in varying degrees.

"It's socialization," I explain to Kamron. "Like when you're a rich, white boy, there are no limits on who you can be. Sure they can be bullied for being autistic, but they're not seen as an embarrassment to whiteness. But when you're a Black girl from Mississippi, autism looks different because everyone around me has made me change myself to be 'less autistic.'"

I put the last part in air quotes because autism is seen as an embarrassment to the Black community—any deviance is. I study his face to see if he understands, but he looks even more clueless.

"It's like code-switching, but nonstop and even with other Black people."

" Oh." He nods sympathetically. "I think I've only met one autistic person. At my old school. He was white, but he would talk about Jeff Dunham, nonstop. This man was obsessed, and I remember watching his stuff on YouTube like this guy ain't even funny." He chuckles.

I grimace. "I don't know who Jeff Dunham is."

He shakes his head. "He's a ventriloquist. He has a doll that he talks to. You're not missing anything...unless you're into that."

I shake my head then giggle, "I'm not, but I have other special interests."

"Like what?"

"So many. Hair, gardening, autism, space, um...I'm absolutely in love with girl groups and British pop. Little Mix is god-tier. Better than Destiny's Child."

Kamron's mouth gapes open at my blasphemous statement.

"I ain't sorry." I laugh at my own reference. "But no, I love British pop and cartoons. I don't know what it is, but cartoons for seven year olds? Fire. Maybe it's the pretty colors."

"Do you watch anime?"

I huff remembering two summers ago when Sam and Luna got high, and Sam made us watch *Naruto* and *Shippuden* as an "Intro to Anime." After watching Sakura fight the puppet man for twenty episodes, I tapped out.

"God, no. It's repetitive and boring."

"*Shippuden* or *Yu-Gi-Oh*? There's better anime than that."

"*Shippuden*. Sam made me watch it."

He nods, "I have some really good recs if you're interested."

"Maybe another time." Or never. I don't know if I can stomach more of that.

"Anyway," I circle back to the subject. "Do you have hobbies?"

He scratches the back of his neck. "Um, not really."

I look him over, feeling like he wants to say something, but he's holding it back. "Come on, everyone has at least one thing they like. I just have a lot."

"It's silly." He shakes his head.

"Nothing's silly." I lean in closer, trying to pull it out from him.

"Well," he glances at me and then down at his laptop. "I um...when the pandemic started and we were quarantined...I um..." He looks from side to side, like someone's watching him. "I started making pottery."

"Really?" My eyes widen. "That's really cool. I always wanted to do pottery."

He lifts an eyebrow. "You don't think it's...corny?"

I scrunch my nose. "Why would I think that? Do you have any pictures?"

He pulls out his phone and shows me the things he made: bowls, platters, and mugs. His face lights up as he talks about his process making them.

"I really want to try this." He goes to his downloads and shows me a teapot set. "Back in California, I had a kiln so it was a lot easier to make stuff, but I brought my wheel. I've been playing around with different projects, you know, tryna see what I can make." He looks up from his phone and to me. "Maybe one day I can expand and learn how to build furniture. I think that'd be pretty cool."

"Yeah, I think you should do it."

He gives me a long look and shakes his head. "I just always thought people would think I was weird or something if I told them that."

"People already think that I'm a weirdo so." I shrug.

His smile softens then his face grows serious. "Has it um...has it been hard, you know, dealing with other people?"

I chew on the end of my thumb nail. "Um...yeah. I mean no one wants to hang out with the weird autistic kid, right?" I laugh nervously then swallow. "Before I was diagnosed, people just thought I was weird, robotic, trying to act white—that was the most offensive because who wants to be white? But people talked to me then. But after I was diagnosed, it was like—" I search for the right word. "Autism has such a big stigma to it. Nobody wants an autistic child or an autistic friend so nobody wanted to be around me except for Sam and Luna." I bite my lip and shrug. It was after my diagnosis that Kennedy and a chunk of my extended family stopped talking to us.

"That's...messed up."

I nod and wrinkle my nose. "It *is* messed up."

I try not to linger on the negative feelings for long, but it's human desire to want to be close to others. To want to be accepted for who we are. Being autistic doesn't mean I'm okay with the isolation and loneliness.

"Well I'm sorry." His gaze meets mine. "If I did anything to make you feel uncomfortable or bad, I didn't mean to."

"Thank you." I give a small smile. "I'm sorry, too. I may not have assumed the best of you." I drop my head and pinch my index finger. "It's just that when people showed interest in me, it was usually to make fun of me."

He offers his hand to me. A peace offering. I glance at it but don't take it. "You didn't deserve that, Naima."

I gaze up at him, searching his face for some sign of malice, but I don't find any. He seems genuine. I squeeze my hands together and sigh. I know I don't deserve the mistreatment, but knowing that doesn't make it easier to deal with.

"Thank you," I say. He smiles. I look down at the supplies on the table. "Do you want to get started?"

The question jolts him, and he remembers what we are supposed to be doing. "Yeah, but are you good?"

"I am." I smile softly, and he returns the smile.

When he clips the lamp on the table, I grab a bottle of water, a packet of yeast and scissors. I add the tiniest pinch of yeast to the test tube and swirl it in a small amount of water. He cuts the elodea and places it in the tube. I fill the rest with water, and we slide the beaker towards the lamp. He sets his timer then we count the bubbles. There are definitely more bubbles than when we added the baking soda. At the first count, our numbers vary by two bubbles. We decide to try four more times since we counted five times during our last experiment.

During our fourth count, I peek at Kamron. He's staring intently at the test tube. His mouth barely moves while he counts. Usually, when I see people, it's only an outline of their body. Like I saw that Kamron was around my height, amber skin with tightly coiled hair that he cut low on the sides and grew out on the top. Faces, on the other hand, are a whole 'nother ballpark. A person's face is usually blank to me. Nothing really sticks out as interesting unless I get the chance to really study it. Even with people I know well, like Sam and Luna, I'm always surprised when I get the chance to actually look at their faces.

Kamron's face is round. His lips are shaped into a little bow. I already knew that because I tend to watch people's mouths move when they talk. Years of doing this though, and I still have not mastered the art of lip reading. His lips are drawn tight in concentration. His wide nose has a rounded tip, and his hooded eyes have dense lashes that curl up at the ends. People pay to have eyelashes like his.

"You have pretty eyelashes," I blurt out. When I realize what I've done, I squeeze my eyelids shut and cover my face with my hand. That was a mistake. Abort. Abort.

"Thank you?" He looks up from the beaker, confused at first, but then his lips slowly open into a smile, and I see how straight his teeth are and how his top teeth graze his bottom lip. He has a pretty smile too. *God, what is wrong with me? Naima. Project. Focus.*

The timer beeps. I jump, clutch my chest, but quickly reorient myself.

"Um, I think—I think we need to do that again. I don't think we got an accurate count."

He grins but agrees. With my elbow on the table, I turn

my head away from him and towards the beaker so I can concentrate on the next two counts. Hopefully, he forgets me completely embarrassing myself and calling him pretty out of nowhere. I hope he also forgets when I called him annoying. Basically, there's a lot of forgetting I need him to do to feel any semblance of comfort working with him again.

We finish our counts and add them to the Google Doc.

"What's next?" I ask.

He scrolls on his computer. "We finish our lab report and create a presentation and then we're good."

"And when's it due?"

He scrolls again. "Um...not this Monday, but the next."

"Do you want to meet again next Thursday and finish it?"

"Yeah. That's fine."

He unclips the lamp and turns it off. I grab the test tube to pour the water out of it and help him pack up. When we finish, I walk him to the door.

"See you tomorrow!" he says as he walks through the door.

He walks across the porch and towards the steps before I remember to add, "Drive safe!"

I shut the door behind me and lean my head against the door. Not only does Kamron know I'm autistic, but I was also being creepy and said he had pretty eyelashes which was a mistake. I'm pretty sure he's gonna tell Mrs. Truss that he wants a new partner, or we're gonna finish this project, and he'll never speak to me again. Do I even want him to speak to me again? I don't know. I thought we were getting along fine, but now? I ruined everything. I slide down the door until I'm sitting and hug my knees into my chest.

Why do I keep embarrassing myself in front of him?

Chapter Eleven

I slide another loc off my hair and onto the bed then undo the plait that the loc held onto. I just finished taking down the back half so I finger detangle it. Luna's face beams when she talks about her date last night with Kike. They drove to Philadelphia to go bowling. She wants me to go with them next time, but I'm not interested in being a third wheel. Instead, I nod and say, "We'll see."

"I know that means no, Naima," she says. I laugh because she's right, but she changes the subject. "Now that I have a date for Homecoming, when are we getting our dresses?"

It's September already. I look away for one second, and a month passes by. The Homecoming dance is in three weeks.

"We should order them today, right?" I ask, while working to loosen another loc from my hair. "I saved a few sites on your computer the last time we looked at dresses."

She opens her laptop and moves the phone around. There's clicking while she's searching for the dresses. She purses her lips as she's deciding between the dresses.

"I think I like this one the best." She turns the camera around for me to see. It's the silky gown that shimmers when you walk.

"Do they still have our size?" I ask.

"What size are you getting? I'm thinking about getting a 12."

I slide the loc off and add it to the pile on the bed. "What do the reviews say? Is it tight? I can't wear a tight dress."

She stares back at her computer screen. "It says it's a little snug but it stretches."

"I'll get a 14 just to be safe. What color are you wearing?"

"If it's star themed, I'm thinking maybe gold or silver. Like a movie star." She clicks the mouse pad. "Ugh, they're out of the gold so I guess I'm going with silver. What color are you getting?"

"I'm thinking like a dark blue." The color of the midnight sky.

She searches for it. "They have it in your size! I'd go ahead and order it."

"Send me the link."

When she does, I click on it, order it with Mom's card, and text Mom that I ordered my Homecoming dress. I get a confirmation email saying the dress will be here within seven to ten business days. We better hope they fit because it doesn't give us a lot of time to send it back.

After Luna finishes ordering her dress, she asks me, "Have

you thought about a date?"

"No," I scoff. "I thought I was going with Sam, but he was on a date last week so maybe I'm fifth wheeling."

"Wait. Sam was on a date? Why did no one tell me?" she leans closer to the screen.

"He didn't tell me. I was just walking on the square, and there he was with some girl at the ice cream place. I have no idea who she was."

"What did she look like?" Luna's eyes widen with excitement.

"Skinny. Blonde."

"Give me a sec," Luna says before her screen goes dark. I finish half of the front of my hair and detangle it before starting on the last quarter of my head. A message pops up on my phone and then Luna's face returns. "Is this her?"

I open the message, and it kind of looks like the girl from the other day. "I think it's her."

"It's one of his groupies!" She laughs while super close to the screen. "That girl commented on every one of his videos for like the last month."

"Sam's fallen off." I shake my head in disbelief.

He used to be a hot boy at our school. In junior high, girls flocked to him. A lot of them used to say I was "lucky" to be such close friends with him, but I had a crush on him, too—for an embarrassingly long time. Back then I confused his affection for romance, but I learned that we can be affectionate with others in a platonic way. I blame the puberty hormones more than the autism for that mixup, but eventually I realized that me and Sam are just friends. Always have been. Always will be.

Luna cocks her head to the side and squints her eyes. "I don't think he's dated anyone all year."

"There was that girl in January. Lexi or something," I struggle to recall.

"Yeah, and they were broken up by Valentine's Day. Wow, Sam really has fallen off."

"He's a loser like us."

She tilts her head down and widens her eyes, like I need to clarify what I just said. "Me and Sam are losers because we're in the trenches."

She laughs, and Kamron's face flashes in my mind. Friday at lunch, he was laughing at the table. He clutched his chest while everyone around him was laughing, even Kennedy. I spiraled wondering if he was talking about me, if Kennedy told him anything, and if he was gonna make fun of me now. He didn't talk to me in AP Bio, but I shake the memory off.

"You okay, girl?" Luna asks.

"I just remembered. I told Kamron that I'm autistic."

Her eyes widen, and her mouth makes an O. "When?"

"A couple of days ago. He was like 'cool.'" Now my eyes widen because what did that even mean? Back when I was diagnosed, my diagnosis spread across town without my permission. I had no control over how others saw me. I was pitied, infantilized, or demonized. When I saw how quickly people changed, I learned to keep my mouth shut about it. But I told Kamron. Maybe some part of me knew that he'd take it well, but there's still the chance that he's like everyone else that'll use my diagnosis to ostracize me.

"Did he do or say anything?"

"I mean he showed me his pottery and stuff, and we talked about my special interests."

"How much did you talk about Little Mix?" she asks.

"I barely mentioned them," I laugh. "I did really good."

"Okay." Her eyebrows pull together as she's thinking. "Maybe when he meant cool, he actually meant that it's cool, and he thinks you're cool."

"Nobody thinks I'm cool."

"I think you're cool." She smiles at me.

"You just said I was a loser!"

"I was joking." She laughs before sobering slightly. "Tell me if Kamron is ever mean to you, and I'll beat him up."

I laugh picturing short Luna trying to fight Kamron. She's like 5 '5.

"I'll let you know." I rake through the last quarter of my hair. "I'm gonna wash my hair, but I'll talk to you later."

"Okay. I love you, and have a good Labor Day." She presses her finger to her lips and to the screen.

"You too! Love you. Bye!" I wave at her and hang up.

I open Spotify and click the Little Mix Mix that the algorithm curated for me. I turn the volume up, tilt the phone by the shower, and start the shower. When I get in, I let the water fall down until my hair is drenched. Holding the ends of my hair with one hand, I use the pads of my fingers to massage the water into my scalp. My eyes roll back because of how amazing it feels.

When "Salute" comes up on shuffle, I squeal. An oldie and goodie. Between copying the girls' dance moves from the videos, I work the shampoo into my hair and scalp. When the lather washes down the drain, I'm left with hair that coils up again. My heart swells. It's like seeing an old friend.

I shampoo my hair again before working conditioner and water into my hair to detangle. I turn the shower off because this takes a while—especially with a month's worth of shed hair. With my duckbill clips, I pin up my hair to work on it a quarter at a time. "Woman Like Me" plays, and it powers me to detangle my entire head.

Rinsing the conditioner out of my hair, I drench my hair with water, reach into my jar of gel, pull out a glob, and work through the back of my hair. Then I drench the front with water and repeat the process. Section by section, I work the gel into my hair until I feel my strands are coated root to tips. When my head is finished, I pin it out of my face, shower, and then throw on a robe and socks.

I walk downstairs to Mom's room.

"Need the hair dryer," I tell her when she looks up from

grading papers.

In her bathroom, by the door is the collapsible hair dryer. I grab it, set it up on the kitchen table, and sit under it to dry my hair. Sitting cross-legged in the chair, I scroll on social media. When I don't find anything interesting, I open random apps until I see the lab doc. I decide to finish working on it. By the time my hair is dry, I finished the introduction, methods, materials, and results section. Now when I meet with Kamron next week, we only need to write the discussion and conclusion.

Mrs. Truss stands at the front of class and lectures about cell signaling. Over the past month, I've learned that while she talks, I'll just rewrite as many words as she says on my paper so I can both stim and look like I'm following along.

"Paracrine signaling" —she writes on the board— "is the signaling that happens between cells that are close together. This signaling usually regulates pain and inflammation."

I write down *paracrine signaling*, *cells close together*, and *pain and inflammation* and then look at my notes because it doesn't seem right.

"Mrs. Truss?" I raise my hand. Before she calls my name, I explain, "Do you mean autocrine signals are responsible for pain and inflammation?"

It's an honest mistake. Maybe she got mixed up because it happens to me. She looks at her paper and then back at me.

"Autocrine signals are the things that kill viruses," I try to explain. "So it would make sense that those would trigger pain and inflammation."

She crosses her arms, and a scowl spreads across her face. "Go to the office."

I don't even fight her because I already know how it's going to play out. I protest. It gets worse. Mom yells at me. I sigh, grab my binder and textbook, and leave. When Mrs. Dean sees me, she shakes her head but leaves me alone. Twice in a month by the same teacher? It has to be a record.

I stare up at the drop ceiling and clasp my hands in my lap. Breathing in through my nose and out through my mouth, I try to calm myself before I get upset or worse. I breathe again and hang my head over my thighs.

"Mrs. Dean, how was your Labor Day?" a familiar voice says. When I look up, I see his smile beaming. It's Kamron.

"It was great. We threw a little something on the grill and the grandkids came over."

"Alexis and Justice, right?" he asks.

"That's right." Although her back is turned to me, I can hear the smile in her voice. "Now I know you're not down here to say hi?"

"No ma'am. I got sent to the principal's office," he says and then looks past her at me. I avert my gaze and cross my arms to tamper the nervousness that's building in my chest.

"You?" she asks with an amount of shock she'd never have for me.

"Yes ma'am. Do I sit back there?" he asks her, pointing towards me.

When she nods, he walks past her desk and sits down beside me. His legs are spread wide. He leans over and rests his elbows on his thighs.

"What did you do?" I ask him. Why would the golden boy be sent to the principal's office?

"You were right." He looks towards me.

"I know I was." I gaze back at him. "What? She sent you here to apologize?"

"Nah. She sent me here because I agreed with you."

My jaw tightens, and I exhale through my nose. I hope he doesn't see me as weak or incompetent just because I told him I was autistic. "I don't need you to save me. I can take care of myself."

He puts his palms out in defense-mode. "No, I believe you. I wasn't trying to save you. Just—" He tilts his head back and forth, measuring his words. "Support you. If you want it."

I lay my head back against the cool concrete wall, close my eyes, and exhale. I wish I could just go one day without getting everything wrong.

Kamron slides back in his chair. "I don't get why she'd send you out for correcting her."

"That's what most teachers do," I explain. "They believe in some made-up hierarchy that because they're older and in a position of power, that they should never be questioned or called out when they're wrong. It's silly. And to make it worse, they're being questioned by someone they think is on the bottom of their hierarchy so every time I'm right, they have an identity crisis."

"That's messed up," Kamron exhales.

"Everything is messed up," I say. I've also been told before that I needed to fix my tone and delivery. But it doesn't matter what I do, people always get offended when I open my mouth.

We sit, staring at the ceiling, and slowly, over the minutes, the anger that rose in my chest subsides. Principal Lewis walks out of his office, sees me, and sighs.

"Who was it this time?" he asks.

"Mrs. Truss," I say.

He shakes his head in disapproval. "And you, young man?"

"It's not his fault. I—I got him in trouble," I speak for him, knowing that me and Principal Lewis have an understanding. Usually, the understanding is that I'm a troublemaker who can't help but find herself outside his office. Kamron should be spared.

Principal Lewis puts his hands on his hip, shifts his feet, and looks down at the floor like he's thinking about our appropriate punishment. How many times had he told me he didn't want to see me again outside his office, yet there I was?

An insubordinate teenager who can't keep her autistic mouth shut.

"Okay," Principal Lewis says and walks away.

We lean back in the chairs and let out a sigh of relief in unison.

Kamron turns towards me. "You didn't have to do that."

"And let the golden boy get in trouble?"

"Is that really how you see me?"

"I mean you're perfect and everyone loves you." I gesture to Mrs. Davis who was just charmed by him minutes ago.

"I'm a lot of things. Funny. Charismatic. Cute."

Add conceited to the list.

"But I'm not perfect. I'd never want to be."

That causes me to sit up and turn towards him. Who wouldn't want to be perfect? He's staring towards Mrs. Davis's back, leaning with his elbows on his thighs.

"What's wrong with being perfect?" I ask.

"It's boring." He grins, tilting his head toward me where I can see his canine hit his bottom lip. I swallow the heat rising in my throat. "And perfection is an unattainable goal. You're working your whole life for something that doesn't exist. It's a waste of time."

Perfection is a waste of time? How can it be? It seems everyone else only likes you if you speak perfectly, act perfectly, dress perfectly, look perfectly. If you don't, you're the odd one out and made fun of for it. Excluded for not being perfect.

If I can never be perfect, then it means accepting that I may always be the odd one out. Always sent to the principal's office for misunderstandings. Always misinterpreting the actions of others.

I exhale and scan my brain for a less depressing way to continue the conversation. "So you're saying you're flawed?"

"Everybody is."

"Really?" I squint disbelievingly. "What's your flaws?"

Having a face too pretty and being too smart for his own good?

"I wear glasses."

Is that even a flaw?

"I do too." I wear blue light glasses so I don't get migraines when I look at computer screens for an extended amount of time. "What else?"

"Um..." He tilts his head to think because he really has to think that hard. Like his flaws aren't top of mind. "I can't sing."

I cackle. "Me either."

But when I have thirty minutes at home alone before Mom and Markese come, I use that alone time to take over the living room, blast music on the TV, and have my own concert. It's the perfect stim to de-stress from the day.

"None of these sound like flaws," I say then shrug. "I don't know. You sound pretty perfect to me."

"Well what are your flaws then?"

"What aren't my flaws?" I ask sardonically.

He chuckles. "No, I'm serious."

"Well for one, I'm a troublemaker." I wave my arm to showcase us here, outside the principal's office.

He hums. "I don't see it that way."

"And how do you see it?"

"You're a badass."

I scoff. "A badass?" I've been called a lot of things. Never that.

"Yeah. Mrs. Truss was wrong and you spoke up about it, and last time—I don't even know what Dustin said—but you told him to shut up and he did. Badass."

I guess I've never seen it that way. That my inability to zip my mouth and pick up on social cues could be seen as not only positive but badass. I grin, then look at him. Awe twinkles in his eyes, and a smile tugs the corner of his lips.

"Thanks," I murmur, knowing that it's too small a word to show my appreciation for how it feels to be seen as something positive for once.

"Of course."

His face studies mine, and I realize that despite working together for the past few weeks, this is the closest we have been to each other. I can smell the remnants of Watermelon Ice Breaker on his tongue and the heat of his body. When I realize that we may have been staring at each other for an uncomfortable amount of time, I turn back to the giant Roman numeral clock on the wall across from us. It's 1:04.

"Um," I gulp. "We have ten minutes til our next class."

"That's fine with me."

I turn back towards him, and he's still gazing at me.

"I forgot to tell you. I like your wash and go," he says.

My hand instinctively reaches for my hair that I forgot I just took down and washed this weekend.

"Thank you," I say, gently tugging a coil and twirling it around my finger.

His mouth slowly curves into a grin, and the look in his eyes makes my cheeks tingle.

Chapter Twelve

When Mom gets home, she calls me downstairs. Sam's a terrible friend who didn't come over to shield me from her, so I must face her wrath alone.

Her purse sits on the kitchen bar that she leans over. "Why did I get a call that you were sent to the principal's office?" she asks.

I exhale. Here I was hoping that Principal Lewis leaving me outside his office meant that he wouldn't call Mom. So much for wishful thinking.

"It was nothing," I explain. "I did what you told me to. I watched my tone and tried to tell Mrs. Truss that something she said wasn't right. She still got mad at me."

I squeeze my thumb and start rubbing my thumbnail while I watch her, waiting for her response. My heart beats in my ears. She shifts her head into her hands.

"Naima, I—" she sighs. "You gotta meet me halfway. I can't keep bailing you out. What are you gonna do when you get to college? Huh? I can't protect you if you—you have to learn to control yourself."

Tears form in my eyes because of how many times we've had this talk. No matter how hard I try to be perfect for her, I fail because I'm a failure and a sorry excuse for a daughter. I lower my head.

"I'll try harder to be normal," I whisper and storm up the stairs to my room.

"Naima!" she calls. "That's not what I meant—"

I shut and lock the door. Hyperventilating, I drag myself to the bed and sob into my pillow. She didn't have to tell me. I could feel how embarrassed she is to have an autistic daughter. How much of a disappointment I am that my brain can't work in a way that's convenient for her and everyone around me. Hell, it's not even convenient for me. I cocoon myself and my body pillow into the blanket until my sobs soften, and I sniffle with each breath. My cheeks are sore, and my eyes burn.

Exhaling, I turn on my back, grab my fidget dodecahedron and stare at the ceiling. Squeezing the dodecahedron, I inhale slowly, count to four, hold my breath for another four seconds, and then exhale for seven seconds. It was a technique Dr. Carpenter taught me years ago when I had therapy with her. I do it again and again until the heaving in my chest softens.

I grab my phone to text Luna when I see an email from Kamron twelve minutes ago:

Just wanted to check on you to make sure you're okay. Let me know if there's anything I can do to help.

I look at the email and wipe a tear from my cheek thinking of a response. Maybe Sam was right about me misinterpreting things. I always assumed the worst of Kamron, but he's continually checked in on me and has been kind to me. I think it's silly but kind of sweet that he still sends me emails. Back when we started working together, he emailed me his number, and I saved it, thinking I may never use it, but why not?

NAIMA: Hey Kamron. Got your email. Feeling much better.

NAIMA: This is Naima btw

While I wait for his response, I tap the screen. He replies within a minute.

KAMRON: I'm glad you're okay. And I've been upgraded to a phone number? I think this means we're friends now.

I smile at the screen and bite my bottom lip. Maybe we are friends now.

NAIMA: We'll see about that

KAMRON: I promise I won't abuse my newfound privilege

I giggle and send him the laughing emoji.

NAIMA: Thank you for today. I appreciate you standing up for me.

KAMRON: Of course. We're friends.

"How are things with your Mom?" Luna asks when we sit down at lunch together.

"She left breakfast for me this morning." Anytime Mom and I are in a disagreement, and she's in the wrong, she makes me food instead of apologizing.

Luna offers a sympathetic smile. "I'm sorry, girl."

I shake my head. Mom wants me to be independent. She wants me to control my behavior. She wants me to overcome my disability which when you're constantly getting messages that autism can be treated or cured, it makes sense that I'm not trying hard enough. I wish she'd believe me when I tell her that I try everyday, but I have limits.

"Hey ladies." Kamron puts his tray down and sits beside me. "What's up?"

Our mouths are wide open trying to process what's happening. I didn't exactly tell Luna that I texted Kamron last night and that he said we're friends now, but she's looking at me with questions in her eyes.

"We...were....just talking...about Homecoming. Right, Naima?" she asks me to confirm.

"Yeah." I smile nervously.

Kamron smiles, too. His perfect smile. "I haven't decided if I'm going or not."

"Really?" she asks. I think we're both stunned that Kennedy hasn't forced him to be her date. "We only have two weeks left. It's basically a prom for underclassmen. You should come."

"I'll think about it," he says to her and then grins at me. My cheeks tingle so I wiggle my toes.

"Kam-Kam, what are you doing over here?" Kennedy stands next to Kamron. "Come back to our table."

He glances up at her. "I wanted to sit over here"—he smiles at us—"with my friends."

She protests, but he offers, "You can sit with us." Then, he looks at us for approval. Luna also looks at me, and I gulp.

"It's up to you, Kennedy." I bite my bottom lip.

She hesitantly sits down beside Kamron, and doesn't say anything, just stirs the chicken and rice on her tray with her fork. The mood shifts. All of us awkwardly eat the food on our tray.

"So," Kamron says, cutting through the silence. "Do y'all know each other?"

"Yeah," Kennedy whispers, avoiding our gaze.

"We used to be friends," Luna explains.

"Best friends," I say, looking at Kennedy while she tucks her head into her chest. Kamron's eyes widen when he begins to grasp the history between us. "How's your mom?" I ask her.

"You know Shayla?" she says. "Still annoying as hell."

Aunt Shayla was loud and overbearing. As kids, she constantly pointed out all of Kennedy's flaws to help her "improve herself," but she also smelled like candied sweet potatoes and gave the best bear hugs. I used to have a hate/love relationship with her.

"Tell her I asked about her. I haven't seen her since—" I couldn't finish the sentence. I hadn't seen her since Dad died, and I was diagnosed with autism. She told Kennedy to stay away from me because she was afraid that Kennedy would catch it. Like that's possible.

"Yeah," she says, her voice strained. She stands up and grabs her tray. "I'm gonna sit at our table if you want to come back," she tells Kamron before walking away from us.

Kamron watches her leave before turning back to us to apologize. "I'm sorry. I didn't realize you had history. She never said anything to me about it."

"She's my cousin," I explain. "Her mom is my dad's sister."

His mouth forms into an O. As the tears form in my eyes, I shake them away. Kennedy made her decision to side with Aunt Shayla instead of me. I don't know why it still bothers me so much that our friendship wasn't enough for her to choose me.

When the bell finally rings, I'm so glad that we don't have to awkwardly talk more about my relationship with Kennedy. Kamron walks with me to class, and instead of sitting in his usual spot near the back, he sits beside me.

"What are you doing?" I ask, smiling.

"We're partners, right?" He returns my grin.

After the bell rings, Mrs. Truss glances up from her notes and scans the class. She grabs her Expo marker and walks to the board. "I hope everyone is here to *learn* today," she remarks, staring at me.

My jaw tightens. I turn to gaze out the window when I feel something brush up against my thigh. When I glance down, it's Kamron offering me his hand. I take it, and he squeezes it.

"I'm here with you. Don't worry." He leans over to whisper. The warmth of his breath sparkles along the ridges of my ear. I really hope he means it.

∘∘∘

After school, I gaze out the window of the Jeep and twirl my hair while I remember Kamron's hand squeezing my palm and interlocking our fingers during class. I don't want to read too much into it and be wrong. I mean I hold Luna and Sam's hands all the time, but it doesn't come with this warmth radiating across my cheeks, chest, and belly.

"So what was that about? With Kamron?" Sam asks once we pass the city limits.

"What was what about?" Can Sam read my mind and does he know about Kamron holding my hand today? Maybe he's a creeper that got out of his class and looked through the door window when I wasn't looking.

"He sat with y'all at lunch and Kennedy was there?" he asks, still looking towards the road

"Oh yeah that." I shake my head to dismiss his worry. "He's on this thing about us being friends, and he wanted to sit with me and Luna at lunch. Kennedy wanted to sit with him so she did...for a little while."

"And are you? Friends with him?"

He just heard about me talking to my cousin for the first time in two years, and he wants to know if I'm friends with my lab partner?

"I don't know. Maybe? He doesn't seem mean," is all I could tell him. I fidget with my fingers and gaze out the window. We're passing the house with the horses, meaning we'll be home in less than five minutes.

"Are you sure he's someone we can trust? I mean he's from California. You know how they are."

"What does that mean?" I scrunch my face.

"Like fake and Hollywood. People who are really good actors."

"You think everyone that lives in California is an actor?" I smirk.

"No, but—" he stammers, tightening his grip on the wheel, "We don't know this guy, and he seems to be—I'm just looking out for you, Nai."

I exhale. Sam has always been super protective of me. As a child, adults would often say, "She's just like that. Bless her heart" to kind of explain why I was a little "off" because none

of us knew what autism looked like in little Black girls
garten was hell for me, because the other kids imm
picked up on my difference and bullied me. Sam threat
beat them up and would play with me during recess so I
alone. I wouldn't have survived if it wasn't for him.

When Dad died and I found out I was autistic, I gue
figured since he was the oldest out of our families, he'd rep
Dad. I've always appreciated him defending me, but I feel
Kamron is different.

"I get that you're worried," I reassure him, "but *you* were th
one who told me that I should get to know him before judgin
him so hard. I think he's okay now. Maybe you should get to
know him too since now you're the judgy one."

We turn into the driveway to my house.

"Fine," he mumbles.

"Awww Sammy's gonna make a new friend, " I say in a baby
voice, pinch his cheek, and grin.

He scoffs. "Quit being weird."

"That's all I know how to be," I sigh, grab my bag, and open
the Jeep door. "See you tomorrow!"

I close the door and walk into the empty house. I'm barely
out of my shoes when Luna video calls me. As I'm rushing up
the stairs to my room, I answer.

"Did you see the way he was looking at you?" Luna squeals
over the phone. Immediately, I know it's about Kamron.
Everyone is thinking about him, apparently. Her shiny brown

eyes stare right into the camera.

"He was looking at me normal," I say to dismiss her giddiness.

I haven't told her about me saying that he has pretty eyelashes or that he stood up to Mrs. Truss for me or that he said he liked my hair or that he held my hand today in class. Now that I'm thinking about it, why am I keeping a list of all the nice things he's said and done for me?

She puts her face right in front of the screen so I could see how serious she is. "If Kike looked at me the way Kamron looked at you today, my legs would be like this." She puts her palms together and then spreads them into a V.

I cover my mouth and throw myself against the bed in a fit of laughter. When it slows, I explain to Luna, "It's not like that. We're just friends."

"Hello! When did you go from he's the most annoying person on the planet to he's my friend?"

I sit back and think about it. I'm not sure. Kamron has always made me feel a lot—mainly annoyance and frustration, but what if it was something else? What if it's friendship?

"Yesterday, he texted me and said that we're friends," I confess, nibbling my inner lip and twirling my fingers. I also accepted his follow request on Instagram and followed him back because that's what friends do.

Luna leans so close to the screen that all I can see are her eyebrows, eyes and nose. "Girl, why didn't you tell me that? I

feel like you're holding out on me. What else did he do?"

"He kinda said that he liked my hair, and he held my hand in class today." Luna's eyes and mouth widen. "No, before you start, it's not like that."

"HE *LIKES* YOU!" she squeals.

I cover my face in my hands. I don't know what's stopping me from believing her. If a boy told her that she had cute hair and held her hands, I would think they were practically married, but why am I so hesitant to believe that about myself? No one's ever liked me for me. I've always had to mask, hide, and silence myself for people to like me. And Kamron's seen the worst sides of me, why would he be interested in me?

Also, what if I think he likes me, and it turns out he doesn't? Then I could risk losing the first friend I've made in years. He could also dump me as a lab partner or sabotage me and my grade if he thinks I'm a creep. I can't afford to misinterpret this.

"You should go to the Homecoming dance with him," Luna says to knock me out of my daze.

"Luna, no!" I tell her. That is the worst idea ever. "He's probably going with Kennedy."

"I don't know." She shakes her head. "He seemed a lot more interested in you than Kennedy."

I scratch my thumbnail and wiggle my toes. I want Luna to be right. The warm tingly feeling vibrating in my cheeks and chest want her to be right. I want him to be interested in me. I want him to like me. I press my palms into my cheeks to try and stop the tingles and tamper down this excitement growing in me. I want to be certain, because feeling these feelings is too much.

CHAPTER THIRTEEN

Luna shows me the makeup she wants to try for Homecoming. It's mostly a nude face but with rose gold eyelids and a lot of highlighter. I tell her it's cute when Kamron joins us for lunch. I guess this is his new routine now. Luna wiggles her eyebrows at me, and I mouth at her to shut up. Seconds later, Sam appears.

"Sam?!" I feign shock, clutching my palm to my chest.

He tightens his lips together and bugs his eyes at me like he wants me to not be weird. Luna laughs then plays along.

"Sam? What are you doing here? Didn't you say you don't want to sit with girls?"

"No Luna." I shift towards her. "I believe his exact wording was, 'I hate those *colored bitches*.'"

Sam's cheeks turn bright red, and I grin. Direct hit. With one hand holding his tray, the other he puts out towards Kamron trying to defend himself against our accusations.

"No, no, no. I didn't say that. I'd *never* say anything like that. Nai, you're joking. She's joking," he says to Kamron, trying to apologize for me.

"Are you sure because you told me, 'Luna, speak American'?" she drawls to pull off his Southern accent.

"Good one," I whisper in her ear. Hearing Kamron snicker is all the encouragement I need to ramp it up. "Yeah, Sam, why would you say something like that?" I blink dramatically.

He shakes his head, sighs, and sits down with his tray. "If I was racist, why are y'all friends with me?"

Luna and I look at each other. Neither of us have a good comeback so I shrug. "Fine, you win."

A smug grin creeps across Sam's face. I try to cover my smile with a scowl.

"Sam, right?" Kamron asks. "Naima said you're really into anime. Like *Naruto*?"

Sam gives a confused smile. "Not exactly *Naruto*. I was just showing them because it's good for beginners."

"I don't know, man," Kamron counters. "I think there are stories with better quality that are less...tedious than *Naruto*."

Not Kamron saying Sam has bad taste. I look from one boy to the other like it's a showdown.

"Okay, but back then, shows came out every week so they could just make episodes for the hell of it, but now shows are shorter so the story stays on track."

"I think it would've been better to start off with *Cowboy Bebop* or *Samurai Champloo*. I don't know if you've seen it, but it's like medieval Japan with 2000s hip hop."

"I've seen them. They're good," Sam admits, "but Naruto has likable characters."

"My favorite was the 'This is a drag' guy," I chime in.

"Shikamaru," they answer simultaneously, staring at each other like they're on opposing sides of a game show.

"Rock Lee and Guy are pretty cool," Sam says.

"When Rock Lee dropped the weights off his feet?" Kamron references. "*That* was badass."

"I'm mad I understood that," Luna says.

"Me too." I shake my head as I see Kamron get Sam's stamp of approval. Looks like we have a new friend in our group.

They keep talking about some more animes and then mangas that I've never heard of and don't care to learn more about. Between bites, Luna checks her email to see when our dresses and her accessories are coming in. Our dresses should be here next week. Hopefully they fit.

"Have you decided on shoes and hair and stuff?" Luna asks.

"I don't know," I shrug. "Maybe I'm just gonna go to the hair store and find something that goes with my dress."

When Luna's eyes widen, I remind her, "I have the dress. That's all I care about."

"Are you ready, Naima?" Kamron asks.

My eyebrows scrunch together as I try to remember what he's talking about.

"Lab?" he says, assessing my confusion. "You forgot, didn't you?"

Yes. Every last drop of my attention went to Mrs. Truss yesterday in class when Kamron was holding my hand.

"Of course, lab. I remember." I look down at the half eaten food on my tray, finish off the peaches and drink my milk, then tell him, "I'm ready."

We grab our trays and stand up when Kamron says, "It was nice meeting you, Sam."

"Yeah, you too."

From Kamron's side, I smile at Sam and nod my head to show that this is good, right? We have a friend and maybe he sees now that Kamron isn't so bad once you get to know him.

When we get to the lab, there's only one other student in class. We sit at the same table we did last month and get started. Today, we're working on a respiration lab. We grab gloves and safety goggles to start assembling the respirometer. Following the directions, I take a respirometer and fill it with twenty mL of water and twenty germinating seeds and record the volume. Kamron takes the other respirometer with twenty mL of water, twenty non-germinating seeds, and enough plastic beads to equal the volume of my respirometer.

We empty the respirometers for the next step where we have to use KOH—potassium hydroxide. When Mrs. Truss sees us grab the bottle, she reminds the class that it's caustic and to not get it on our skin. Kamron slides the absorbent cotton to the bottom of each respirometer. I carefully add drops of KOH to each respirometer until the cotton ball is noticeably wet. Then

Kamron uses a stick to slide a ball of non absorbent cotton on top of the wet cotton ball. I add the germinating seeds back to mine, and Kamron adds the non-germinating seeds and beads back to his. We add the stoppers on top.

We have to measure respiration in an ice bath so Kamron goes to the front of the room and grabs ice out of the cooler near Mrs. Truss, adds water to it, and brings it back to the table. We lean the respirometers on the ice to let the temperature equalize and set a timer for five minutes to wait. I take my gloves off and rest my head on my hands when I see Kamron gazing at me.

I scrunch my eyebrows. "What?"

"Nothing." He shakes his head. "I just remembered we have to finish our outside lab. It's due Monday."

I completely forgot. Thankfully, I wrote half the report over the weekend.

"Are you free tonight?" I ask.

"Yeah. Same time?"

I nod and then glance at the timer. Still two minutes to go before we can submerge the respirometers.

"Hey, I'm sorry if I got you in trouble the other day. You gotta be careful of the cart you hitch your dragon to." That's not right. "The car you hitch your wagon to. The cart—"

A snicker slips from Kamron's lips when he fails to hold in his laugh.

"I know I'm saying it wrong." I blink. "I love idioms; I'm just so bad at them. I feel like a bad Southerner."

"I think it's 'the horse you hitch your wagon to' and it's okay. My aunt doesn't really care what I do."

"That must be nice." Meanwhile Mom cares about every single little thing I do.

"If I stayed with my grandparents, it'd be a different story, but Amaya's cool. She's the rebel in our family."

A rebel? That's intriguing. "How?"

"She um...didn't go to college. She's a mechanic, and she married a woman. Didn't work out, but—it gives my family something to fight over on the holidays."

I smile. Are all families messy with someone hating someone else for how they show up in the world? The timer goes off, and we submerge the respirometers into the ice bath and set the timer for four minutes.

I mine what we just talked about to keep the conversation going. "What would it have been like to stay with your grandparents?"

"They whew—" he exhales. "They're old school. They want you to have perfect grades, perfect attendance, perfect behavior. My grandma yelled at me when I was ten or something cause I walked in a room and didn't speak to everyone in that room." He shook his head.

"Perfect's overrated," I say, referencing his comment from a few days ago.

Maybe he's right. Perfect is unattainable. Even though my

grades are excellent, my disability is always the asterisk. The thing I must overcome to truly be seen as Black excellence. Pretending to be neurotypical long enough to make others comfortable comes at such a high cost to me that I wonder if people actually care about me, the Black person, or the product, excellence.

"It is, but I understand where they're coming from. If they weren't perfect, they would be harassed or beaten. It was a different world for them. California wasn't the liberal haven people make it out to be. Even in the big cities."

California? Were they born there or here? Did they ever live in Mississippi? "How did they end up in Mississippi?"

The timer goes off after I ask the question, but I wave at him to keep talking while I check the respirometers, record the measurement, and restart the timer.

"Yeah, they were born in Mississippi. After they got married, they moved out to San Francisco."

"And you were born in Sacramento?"

"Yeah, my Mom was born in San Francisco, moved to Sacramento after she married my Dad, had me and my sister. My grandparents moved back to Mississippi after they retired."

"So your aunt and your mom are sisters and your aunt moved here when?"

"She moved in with her grandparents. My great-grandparents."

"Okay," I say while my brain sorts through his family tree.

"I'm sorry if it feels like I'm prying. I was just curious about when people leave Mississippi, why do they come back? We had to do a genealogy project a few years ago, and my oldest ancestor lived in Mississippi in the late 1700s—before Mississippi was a state. So this is basically the only home my family's known for centuries."

"You're not prying," he reassures me. "And that's pretty cool that you can track that far back."

I guess cool is one word for it.

"It's hard to imagine what it must've been like for them. To stay," I admit.

I know that I go hard for Mississippi, but I have to because after all the blood and tears that soaked into this soil, my ancestors made this state their home. I've always wondered why and if they ever regretted the decision to stay. Why did those that leave want to come back?

"My family's kinda like yours," I say. "My grandma's sisters—I've never met them—but they moved after they graduated college. One lives in San Francisco. The other Chicago, but my grandma stayed here."

"That Mississippi to California pipeline," he remarks.

"Yeah like Snoop Dogg."

He snorts, and Mrs. Truss sends us a warning glare. The timer goes off again, and this time Kamron bumps into me to turn it off. His knee touches mine while he reads the respirometer and records the measurement. My chest flutters, and I think about pushing his leg away, like maybe it's a mistake, but surely he feels it too. Maybe it's on purpose. Maybe he wants it there.

When he restarts the timer, he wants me to keep talking, but I'm kind of tired of the discussion and instead want to circle back to the idea of perfection.

"Can I ask you a question? It's kind of controversial," I wrinkle my nose in anticipation of his answer.

"Sure."

"What do you think of Black excellence?"

He sucks the air in through his teeth. "That is a controversial question."

With my head held up by my arm, I giggle as I watch him ponder it.

"Well, my dad would always tell us 'You gotta work twice as hard to get half as much' and I get that. My parents have done alright for themselves, and I appreciate everything their hard work has given me, but sometimes I just be tryna live and they act like if I'm not succeeding 24/7, it's like my life means nothing."

I find myself smiling at him and his answer. That's exactly it. Why does my life have to be constantly defined by my ability to succeed? Why can't I just live?

"That's beautiful. I'm just tryna live," I repeat the words to myself.

What really makes a life? Is it constant success or is it these small moments that we get to experience with each other? I look up at Kamron who's peering into my eyes. Despite the way his gaze stings my chest and my cheeks, I stare back. There's something about eye contact that's so intimate. Staring into someone's eyes is to be a witness to their existence. Returning their gaze is to allow them to be a witness to mine. It's a vulnerable exchange—a reminder that we are both alive and sharing this moment together.

The timer goes off and we shuffle, moving towards the table. His knee grazes my thigh, but I don't say anything. Instead, I look at the respirometer, clear my throat, and tell him what it says so he can write it down. He restarts the timer, and we both watch it until it goes off. I rub my earlobe until it's time to take our last measurement. After we do, we start cleaning up our station. He dumps the ice out, and I throw the respirometers' contents in the trash.

When the bell rings, he says, "See you tonight."

I smile, press my binder into my chest, and walk off to my next class.

I'll see him again tonight.

CHAPTER FOURTEEN

Holding a cup of rooibos tea, I stand on the porch. The cicadas hum while I wait for Kamron. This is the only way that I can avoid talking to Mom. Since Tuesday, I've been hiding out in my room after school, only coming out to grab dinner and then rushing back. Kamron pulls up five minutes till five. When he parks, he pops a mint in his mouth before flinging his bookbag over his shoulder and walking towards me. I offer a tight-lipped smile and a wave, but his smile widens enough for his teeth to graze his lips. I clear my throat to loosen the sudden tightness.

"Didn't get lost again, did you?"

Oh my god, Naima. Is that the best you can come up with? This is like his fourth time coming over. I forcibly blink away the embarrassment, but he chuckles.

"Nah. I'm getting pretty good at finding the place. Didn't even have to use GPS this time."

"That's good," I say, opening the door for him to pass by.

We sit at the kitchen table, and Mom's standing at the bar.

While Kamron pulls out his laptop and plugs it in, she asks if we need any drinks or snacks. I lift my mug and avert my gaze. I don't want her thinking I want to talk to her anytime soon. Kamron tells her that he's fine, and she leaves us alone.

"This may be wildly inappropriate, but it feels like you and your mom—" Kamron says.

"Yeah." I gnaw my inner lip. "She's never happy when I get in trouble at school."

"I'm sorry about that."

"This is actually not your fault." Unlike the first time when he, Dustin, and Mrs. Truss were definitely to blame. This time was also Mrs. Truss's fault, but apparently teachers are faultless angels who never do anything wrong.

"Do you want me to talk to her?"

"No," I scoff.

"Moms love me." He smiles, and I wonder if moms feel the same way about his smile as I do.

"I don't know how you talking to her is gonna help."

"How about this?" He clears his throat and then loudly says, "Wow, Naima you're so smart. I'm so lucky to have you as my lab partner. I'd completely fail this class if it wasn't for you."

I cover my mouth to muffle my laughter.

"Was that good?" he whispers. "Maybe I could add. 'She's certainly not a delinquent.'"

I giggle. "I think that's enough. She's gonna think I put you up to it."

"Okay, then I'll say: 'She did not put me up to this.'"

"Yeah." I nod. "That's really good. Very convincing."

My mouth spreads into an unbelievably wide grin and so does his. When I realize that I may have been staring at him for too long, I grab my mug and bring it up to my lips. Once I sip the tea, I ask about the lab report.

He opens the laptop and pulls up the Google Doc. "I saw you filled out most of the lab report. I'm not kidding. You make me feel like I'm not pulling my weight."

"I had free time this weekend, so I figured I'd just work on it." I shrug.

"I finished the lab report. You can read over it if you want."

He lowers the brightness of the screen and turns the computer towards me. I read over it and notice how he cleaned up my text, fixing my typos and run-ons, but also how clean his copy is.

"Looks good," I tell him when I finish reading. "And we just copy and paste that into Google Slides?"

"Pretty much."

We make slides out of each section. There are a few sections for the experiments and the data. After debating between hyper realistic photos and illustrations, we decide to use illustrations for the pictures. We read over each slide again, checking for typos and double-checking to make sure the information is correct. When it's to our liking, we decide that we'll alternate slides when it's time to present. Kamron emails the presentation to Mrs. Truss, CCs me, and closes his laptop. We've officially finished our first outside lab.

"Is it cool if I hang out here?" Kamron asks.

It takes me a while to answer because I'm surprised by his request. He usually leaves when we're done, but I guess now that we're "friends," we can hang out. Markese is yelling and playing *Fall Guys* with his door open upstairs.

"Yeah. Do you want to go outside?"

He agrees, so I grab a throw blanket from the couch and follow him out the back door.

The buzzing cicadas greet us as we walk on the back porch. The setting sun casts shades of orange, pink, and yellow on the horizon. We sit on the porch swing on the side of the house, and I look out to the corn stalks. The humid air drapes us.

"I've been thinking about what you and Luna said," Kamron starts, "About going to Homecoming?"

"Yeah. Are you going?" I wrap the blanket around me.

"Kennedy asked me, but I told her no." He rubs his palms together. "I don't know if I want to be friends with her. Especially after how she treated you."

"Oh." I chew my inner lip. "I don't—you don't have to do that for me."

"Yeah, I know, but I want to." His smile is closed, showing a hint of a dimple. How does he have such a perfect face? "Were you two close?"

I nod. "Before Luna moved here, it used to be me, her, Sam,

and my other cousin, Eric. And every summer we used to play together out there." I point backwards to the patch of land between mine and Sam's house. "We even went to a Little Mix concert together."

"Oh, that band you claimed is better than Beyoncé?"

"I didn't say better than Beyoncé," I clarify. "I said better than Destiny's Child. There's a difference."

He squints to hint that he doesn't believe me.

"But anyway," I smile, remembering the story, "I heard Little Mix was coming to New Orleans. It was the first—and now I realize only—tour they did in the US, and I begged my dad to take me. Kennedy was a huge Ariana Grande fan—she probably still is—and Little Mix was opening for her. And she also begged Dad to take us, and he did, even though it was a school night. When we got there, I was under the same roof as Little Mix, and it was like I was complete. Like I've heard every single song they sang and watched all their interviews and here I am seeing the real life people. It. Was. Magical."

I shake my head and smile. I live streamed their last show a few months ago. Seeing these women who had been such an instrumental part of my life filled my heart with joy. And even though they're broken up or "on hiatus," I'm so glad I got to be a part of their journey.

"Like I'm so glad they exist, and I got to experience them," I tell him.

I turn over to look at Kamron, and he's just staring at me. I probably lost him a while ago so I clear my throat and get back on topic.

"Um, the concert was good and once Ariana Grande came on, the noise was too loud and the lights were too bright so I had to tap out, and Dad had made friends with these college students there. I think they were like the only adults in our section. Their names were" —I close my eyes to try and remember it— "Catherine and Leah. And they were really nice and Leah offered to sit outside with me because my head was banging and when we got back to school, all Kennedy talked about was seeing Ariana Grande, and I felt bad because I missed most of her set." I sigh. "I'm sorry. That's my favorite memory, but it's also kinda sad."

"No, I'm glad you felt comfortable enough to share that with me. I'm honored." He places his hands over his heart and smiles.

I pull the blanket tighter around my arms and rock.

"I wanted to ask you about your garden." Kamron points to the backyard. "I see it every time I come over. And I was just wondering...do you really grow food?"

I snicker at his silly question. "Yeah. I grow food."

"By yourself?"

"Yeah." I nod, shocked that he thinks it's hard. "Come on."

I stand up and wait for him to join me. Turning on my phone's flashlight, we walk down the stairs to the little plot of land I grow food on. In the front are a row of sunflowers to encourage the pollinators to pollinate my food plants. I squat and touch a thick brown vine. "This gave me about five tomatoes before it was done."

"Here." I turn to the row beside it. "I got a bunch of green beans from this. We ate them on Labor Day, actually."

Kamron squats down with me, turning the thin greenish vines over in his hands. I stand up and take a couple more steps. I point to a bunch of purple triangular leaves. "These are my sweet potatoes. They should be ready soon. And this" —I turn my flashlight to the indentation amongst the yellowing leaves on the ground— "is where I grew my watermelon."

"You grew a watermelon?" he asks, eyes wide.

"It was really good." I smile, proud of my work. "And of course, this" —I point to the stalks— "is corn."

His hands run over the stalk, studying the broad green leaves. I see an ear that is pretty done and pull it off. "You can have this if you want?" I offer it to him.

"No, no." He waves his hands, "I don't want to take your corn."

"It's just corn. You can try it. Tell me how it tastes."

"Thanks." He grabs it. "So what made you start gardening?"

"Um...my dad." I gulp and clutch the blanket tighter. We walk back towards the porch. "When I was younger, he wanted a garden so bad. It was a lot bigger than the one I have now. I thought the same as you when the garden grew. Like we put a seed in the ground, and it grew into food? It blew my mind." I laugh, remembering my awe that first summer we had a garden. How Dad had us drag bags of compost and soil to the garden. How hot it was and how much we complained. But also, how much it was worth it when we took our first bite of the food we made.

I nibble my bottom lip. "I guess—I guess I keep the garden going because if it's still here, so is he."

Looking back at my garden that's about a quarter of the size of his, I may not have always liked the work, but it was one of those things that we regularly did together. It was one of the few things that brought us joy.

"I think he'd be proud of you."

My attention turns back to Kamron who stands on the top step. He offers his hand to me to help me up the stairs. I take it and share a small smile. "Thanks."

We return to the porch swing and sit close enough that our thighs touch. I rock the swing remembering the last time I saw Dad. Mom was making a casserole and forgot cheese, the most important part. Dad offered to drive into town. He didn't even say bye to us because he was so sure he'd be back. We were so sure he'd be back.

After an hour, he still wasn't home. Mom was about to get in the car herself and find Dad, when the police called saying he hit a deer, and like that, I didn't have a dad anymore. He was gone. In a year where 350,000 Americans died from a novel virus, my dad died in a car accident. It seemed there was no room to grieve because everyone else had it so much worse.

A tear falls down my face from the memory. I wipe it away and sniffle.

"You good?" he asks.

"Sorry." I shake my head. "I'm a mess."

When he gently wipes the tear from my cheek, I touch the damp streak it leaves.

"I don't think you're a mess." He ducks his head to enter my line of sight. When I look at him, he smiles. Goosebumps spread across my chest. "I wasn't trying to overstep—"

"No, it's not that." I shake my head again. "I just thought about the last time I saw my dad. He died in a, um...a car accident. We did all this work to avoid getting Covid, and he died because of a fucking deer." I bury my face in my hands.

I didn't even get to see him again. Because of social distancing, we couldn't have a funeral or see the body. He was gone. Forever.

Kamron rubs my arm, and it soothes a lot of the dread. I gaze up at the sky, the stars twinkling.

"You know," I sniffle and wipe a tear away. "When I was younger, I used to think we turned into stars when we die. Like it made sense. If Heaven and angels were in the sky, why wouldn't the stars be the people who went to Heaven? I—" I bite my bottom lip. "I hope that Dad is a star. That although he doesn't exist here with us, he still exists in the universe."

"Hmmm," Kamron hums. "Kinda like how energy is never

created or destroyed?"

"Exactly!" I smile, happy we're on the same page. "Did you know that it takes years for the light from the stars to reach us, so by the time we see it, the star itself could be gone? It's like the star exists and doesn't exist at the same time? And maybe that's how death is. We exist and don't exist at the same time."

"Like memories?"

"Yeah, like memories. That's exactly it! Like we exist in someone's memory which is real, which is an existence, but we also don't. We are not the same as we were in those memories. We evolve and change, but also memories are fallible, so there's that. And the light that we see from the stars are the memories of the stars themselves."

My heart swells as I stare back up at the night sky. This is the first time that someone's given me the space to talk about my dad and death. Anytime I brought it up to Luna or Sam, they froze—like they were tired of me talking about him, but they couldn't say anything to the girl whose parent died. Mom got harder on me, and Markese retreated into video games. It's why I started visiting Dad at his grave. It was the only chance I got to talk to and about him. Sitting here with Kamron now, I don't feel the raw vulnerability that comes with talking about Dad. Instead, it's a release. I feel understood. Seen.

"Naima?"

He lays his hand on top of mine. I look at it and then back up at him. The distant smell of watermelon ice breaker is on his tongue. His face is so close to mine that I can feel his breath on my lips. My eyes travel from his lips to his eyes which are as sure as mine. When his hand reaches around my waist, bringing me closer to him, I do it. I lean over to fill the gap between us and kiss him. My first kiss. His beautiful lips are as soft as I suspected, and he grabs my nape, pulling me closer to him when—

"Nai!"

I jump back and clutch my chest. My heartbeat races as Sam's heavy footsteps come up the stairs and drag across the porch. We stare at each other with faces full of something akin to guilt.

"Nai?"

"I'm back here," I call from the side of the house.

"Nai, I need your help with. Oh," Sam says once he sees Kamron.

Kamron turns back to me. "I'm gonna go. Thank you...for the corn." He waves the ear in the air. "Good seeing you again, Sam."

I wave goodbye to Kamron. When the car door shuts, I let the breath I'm holding go.

"What's that about?" Sam asks, pointing in the direction Kamron left.

"Nothing. What's wrong, Sam?" I try to muffle the devastation in my voice.

"Homecoming's in two weeks, right?" He sits down on the

swing and grabs my hands. "I kinda need your help picking a suit."

My eyes widen, and I lightly slap his arm. "Sam, no. How do you not have your suit already?"

"I was waiting on y'all to pick your dresses so we can coordinate. You know how long girls take to get ready." He playfully rolls his eyes.

"I know you're not talking. We always have to wait for *you*, Mr. Wait till the Last Minute." I grab my phone from my pocket. "Let's hope we can find you a suit before the dance."

When I find a decent site, I give him the phone to look for a suit. While he's scrolling, I touch my lips and remember the warmth of Kamron's kiss.

Chapter Fifteen

Luna squeals when I tell her what happened. "Your first kiss! See? I told you he likes you. How was it?"

I exhale. Not long enough. "It barely got started before Sam showed up and ruined everything."

"Where's your friend?" We look up from each other as Sam walks to our table and puts his tray down. Speak of the devil, and he shows.

I glance around the cafeteria when I realize that I haven't seen him at all today. "I don't know, actually. Have you seen him?" I ask Luna.

She shakes her head. "He wasn't in Pre-Cal this morning."

When I look over at Kennedy's table, neither of them are there. They aren't together, right?

"I guess he realized *Naruto* was the superior anime and left," Sam says with a smug grin on his face.

"I don't think that was it *at all*," I say.

Sam shrugs and manages to con Luna into helping him look for a suit. Most of the ones I showed him last night, he "liked" but didn't "love" so we ended our search empty-handed. I pull my phone from my hoodie pocket to see if Kamron texted me to say he wasn't coming. There's no text or email from him. He hasn't missed a day of school yet so I hope he's okay.

Once I get to AP Bio, he isn't there by the time the bell ring, so I text him.

NAIMA: Are you ok? You're not in class.

I check my phone between each class, and there's still no response from him. He usually messages right away. Did I do something wrong? Is Kamron avoiding me because I entirely misread the situation when I kissed him? I thought he kissed me back, but maybe he was just being nice to me so I wouldn't feel embarrassed, and now he's skipping school to avoid telling me that when he wanted to be friends, he meant just friends.

When we get home, Mom is already parked in the driveway. She's still trying to make up for earlier this week, and I really can't deal with it today. Not now.

"I wanna go to your house," I tell Sam.

He backs out of the driveway and turns onto the dirt road right beside it. When I walk to his room, I sit my bookbag down on the floor, plop in his computer chair, and pull my knees into my chest. He lays flat on the bed with his knees in the air. I zone out focusing on every detail of last night. I must've missed something. How could Kamron go from someone who was really excited to be my friend to someone who leaves me on read?

It had been a week since I told him I'm autistic. I thought he took it pretty well. He seemed to have liked me. He even stood up to Mrs. Truss and held my hand in class. That had to mean something, right? Maybe last night I was talking too much about Little Mix. I tend to talk too much about Little Mix and that drove him away. He said he was honored to hear me talk about it but what does that even mean? He probably made it up so I didn't feel stupid. I look at my phone again, but this time there's a text.

KAMRON: Naima, I'm extremely sorry. I didn't mean to hurt you.

I sit up in the chair. What does he mean "hurt me?" What did he do? I think back to today. He was missing, but so was Kennedy. Does that mean he lied about not wanting to be around her? Did they sneak out today and hook up or something?

NAIMA: Is this about Kennedy?

KAMRON: Yes. I completely understand if you never want to talk to me again.

I stare at my phone. It was silly to assume that he'd like me, that anyone could like me. And I kissed him? Just completely put myself out there and failed spectacularly. Why couldn't I see the signs that when he said he wanted to be friends, he meant just friends? Just because he was being nice to me doesn't mean he liked me. I was too eager, too much, and now I've chased him away.

He really wanted Kennedy, and how could I blame him? Everyone wants her. She's pretty and popular and normal. Why would I think someone like Kamron would ever like someone like me? Nobody could like me.

"You okay?" Sam asks. He peeks from behind his phone. I shake the haze away from my brain.

"Yeah, I'm fine. I'm gonna go home now." I stand up and grab my bookbag.

"We just got here," Sam whines.

"Talk to you later," I call from the hallway on the way out the door.

My breath shallows as I race to my house. All I need to do is make it to my room, and I'll be okay. When I open the door, Mom is sitting on the couch.

"Naima, can we talk?" She clicks the TV off.

I hide my face from her so she can't see the hurt.

"Can't Mom. Really busy."

I run up the stairs, lock my door, crank my music, and put on my noise canceling headphones. At first, I sit up in my bed and hug my knees into my chest. A tear falls from my eyes, and I quickly flick it away. I try to think of anybody, anything, but all I can see is Kamron's perfect face and the way he smiles at me. How could it all be a lie? How could I not see through it? The tears stream down my face, and I tuck my head into my knees to muffle my sobs. My chest tightens, and I rock trying to loosen it up. My jaw grows sore, and my nose stops up so I breathe through my mouth before I scream and weep. I know I messed up because I hear footsteps coming up the stairs.

"Naima." Mom knocks on the door. "Are you okay?"

"I'm fine," but the croak in my tear-stained voice gives it away.

"Can I come in, please?"

I don't want to talk to her, and I don't want her to see me like this, but I also know I need to be held. I need to be told that I'll be okay, that I'll get through this. I go and unlock the door without opening it. I curl into a blanket on my bed and wait for her to walk through it. She opens the door and hesitantly walks over to the foot of my bed. I grab a pillow to pull into my chest.

"Baby, I'm sorry," she apologizes and tries to reach across the bed for my foot, but it's tucked under me. "I don't want you to ever think for a second that I don't think you're perfect just the way you are. There is *nothing*" —she looks me in the eyes— "that I want you to change about yourself."

I nod. It helps that she apologized, but I still feel so small, so insignificant and unseen. Even the fact that she thinks I'm crying about her adds to the invisibility.

She scoots closer to me and uses her thumbs to wipe my tears away. "I'm sorry I did this to you," she says.

I shake my head to signal that this isn't her doing.

"Oh." She understands. "Well I'm sorry that I added on to whatever you're dealing with. You can talk to me about it later if you want." Her voice softens to try and make it seem like a friendly offering.

I doubt Mom wants to hear about me embarrassing myself by kissing a boy I was stupid enough to have a crush on and who obviously didn't like me. She presses my head into her chest and holds me like I need her to. I start crying again and dampen her t-shirt, but she continues to rub my back and shush me. When my tears slow, she kisses me on my forehead and tells me she loves me. I want it to be enough to bandage the sea of unworthiness in me, but it's not. It may never be.

Luna walks into my room late Sunday morning on video call. "Cannonball" plays on my smart speaker while I'm cocooned under a blanket wallowing in my sorrow.

"I found her," Luna says.

"So she's not dead?" Sam's voice comes through the phone.

"Nope."

I grunt, too sad to string words together to speak. Luna lays behind me in the bed and tries to put the phone in my face so Sam can see me. "She's just being dramatic," Luna tells him.

When "Cannonball" repeats, Luna asks, "Have you been listening to this all day?" She puts the phone in front of her face. "Okay, maybe this is an emergency," she informs Sam.

"You need me over there?"

"No, I think I can handle it." She ends the call and wraps her arm around me. "Hey," she whispers into my back. "What's wrong, Naima?"

She inserts her fingers into the base of my hair and rubs my scalp the way I like it. My eyes are dry, and my throat's tired from crying all weekend. I shake my head.

"How about we play a different song? Let's start there," she says slowly.

I pick my phone up from under the covers and select "These Four Walls." I sit in the pain and hurt from their voices because it's too much to try and sift through mine.

"So today's a sad Little Mix day? Got it." She tugs my shoulders to try and get me to turn around and face her. Begrudgingly, I do. "Is this about Kamron? I'm sure he was just sick or something on Friday."

I shake my head again. My face scrunches even though tears won't form in my eyes.

"Naima." Her hand cups my face. "What happened?"

I show her the text messages that Kamron sent me. As she holds the phone in her head, her eyebrows draw together. "It doesn't really make sense."

I emote my best *Exactly!* face.

"I thought he really liked you. He seemed so honest."

I bury my face in my pillow and huff. I thought he really liked me too.

Luna rubs my back. "I get it, but you gotta keep us in the loop. You can't ignore us like that. Sam said you ran out of his house and ghosted."

I lay on my back, inhale slowly, then exhale. Luna mimics me, reaches down to grab my hand, and squeezes it. "I can stay with you all day if you need me to."

I squeeze her hand right back. We lay there until my eyes and body grow heavier. I curl up and drift off to sleep. When I wake up from my nap, Luna's gone. I check my phone, and she texted me that she's downstairs.

NAIMA: I'm up.

Luna reemerges in my door with junk food. I'm grateful because I don't remember the last time I ate. "Feel better?" she asks.

"Yeah," I say quietly. My voice is still waking up from my nap.

She holds up the pint of pistachio ice cream from the freezer. "Got you a treat. Wanna watch Food Network?"

She plops down beside me and grabs the remote from the nightstand. There's a rerun of Ina Garten's show, and we watch her roast a chicken and make a tart for her friends. Handing me a tiny spoon, I start on the pistachio ice cream. I turn the bite of ice cream over in my mouth, letting it slowly melt away until all that's left are the bits of pistachios. Although I love the taste of pistachio ice cream, I hate the textures of nuts. I grab a Kleenex from the side of the bed and spit the nuts in there.

As the show winds down, Ina thanks her friends for coming

over. I kiss Luna's cheek, lay my head on her shoulder, and thank her for digging me out of my funk.

She looks up from her phone. "Of course, girl. I can't have you over here crying over a boy."

"But he's a pretty boy," I sigh. "And he's smart. And he was nice to me." Or I thought he was being nice to me.

"He is pretty," Luna agrees, "But fuck him for treating you like that."

I gnaw my inner lip. Maybe I should feel mad about Kamron like she does, but I just feel sad and hurt. Luna looks back at her phone. "Oh shit."

"What?" I lift my head from her shoulder, and she shows me an email from the school:

Dear Parents & Students,

There have been a number of students who have recently tested positive for Covid-19. Because it is impossible to assess all interactions that a student has, the entire school is considered close contacts. Each student must follow quarantine instructions and stay home from school for 14 days. All classes will be switched to online only. Students should be receiving emails from their teachers soon.

We realize that this quarantine coincides with Homecoming. Unfortunately, there will be no Spirit Week, but we will still have the Homecoming dance. Students will be required to wear masks indoors at all times during the dance.

If you have further questions, please contact Principal Lewis.

"No Spirit Week," I say to Luna. Spirit Week is the best part of Homecoming because we get to dress up everyday. It's basically a whole week of Halloween.

"And virtual classes. Do you want me to stay the night? I can now." She wiggles her eyebrows.

"Yes please," I smile and snuggle closer to her as the Guy Fieri show starts.

⎯⎯ℓℓ⎯⎯

Thankfully, Monday morning our teachers are as discombobulated as we are. They're not requiring any Zoom lectures, just readings and homework that we can email in. Luna and I sit on the couch and work on our homework for the day. We finish by eleven then Sam asks to come over. I meet him at the door wearing a mask and handing him a rapid test. Luna and I tested negative last night.

"Why do I have to do this?" Sam asks, holding the box in the air.

"You could be the one who shut down the school. Who knows?"

He rolls his eyes but opens the box and sits down in a chair. I keep my distance while he swabs his nose. He tries to do a quick swab, but I remind him, "Fifteen seconds. Each nostril."

He huffs but acquiesces, swabbing each nostril until he's about to sneeze.

"What now?" he asks.

"In the solution. Swirl it around, squeeze it, and three drops." I mime the instructions from six feet away. He follows the directions and when he places the three drops on the test, I set the timer on my phone for fifteen minutes. His leg bounces while he waits, and I stand by the door with my arms crossed, watching the timer slowly count down to zero. When it buzzes, he lifts the test annoyed. There's only the control line visible.

"See?" He shoves the test in my face and walks in the house.

"It's better to be safe than sorry." I take off the mask, follow him inside, and close the door.

"Luna?" he calls to her, dragging his feet across the kitchen floor. She turns around to face him.

"When you going back home? You wanna come over?" He wiggles his eyebrows. Why is he trying to steal my friend from me?

"Did you even finish your homework, Sam?" I ask him.

He scoots next to Luna. "We're on vacation. We can do whatever we want now."

"School is still a thing," I remind him sitting on the other side of Luna. "*We* already finished our homework." I point back and forth between me and Luna.

"Good, so you can come over." He presses his palms together in a prayer towards Luna. "I have to squeeze in all I can before baseball season starts."

"I don't see why I can't go over for a few minutes," she says, looking apologetically at me. "I mean I have to go home tonight."

"But you came to see me," I whine, leaning back into the couch.

"And you're doing so much better. It's a reward for my job well done." Her and Sam get up so I splay out on the couch in protest. She follows him to the door. "I'll be back. You'll be fine, Naima."

But will I?

"You're a bunch of...of..."—I scramble to find a word—"delinquents."

Delinquents. It's what Kamron said I wasn't last week. The thought squeezes my heart, because I want to see him again and talk to him but he's with Kennedy. I exhale loudly then leap from the couch. Pacing in front of it, I remember the last thing Kamron said to me. My name. What was he gonna say?

Naima, I like you.

Naima, you're annoying. I groan remembering when I called him annoying.

Naima, shut up. You talk too much.

Naima, you're smart and amazing and perfect. He'd never say that.

Naima, I think I want Kennedy and not you.

Naima.

He touched my hand. The warmth of it still radiates on my skin and tingles up my arms.

Naima.

What was he trying to say? Maybe if I can figure that out. I can figure out why he would go back to Kennedy. Did he do it because I kissed him? I got caught up in the moment and completely violated his physical boundaries, and now he's with someone else. What did I expect to happen?

Standing in the living room, my stomach growls so I grab a Lunchable from the fridge and head up to my room. I plop on the bed, grab my phone and switch from app to app eating the tiny sandwiches. YouTube. TikTok. Instagram. When I open Instagram, I see Kamron's profile, but there's a green ring around it. He made me a close friend? Maybe it was a mistake. Maybe it was from the one week that we were friends. I tap my fingers on the screen before I decide to just look at it. He wouldn't make me a close friend if he didn't want me to see it. Right?

It's a video with the caption: taking advantage of quarantine. His hands are smoothing out clay on a wheel. One hand cups the ball of clay while the other rests on top of it. He adds water to it and continues smoothing out the clay. The wheel keeps turning and then the video ends. I watch it again and again until I hear the door downstairs open. I hide the phone under me like Luna is gonna know what I'm doing. She's not. I sigh then walk downstairs. I'm just looking at his story. It's completely innocent. But he can see that I saw his story. Shit.

I wince.

"You okay?" Luna asks. I can smell her from the staircase.

"No. Fine," I say. "Just forgot my Lunchable."

I spin on one foot and do a 180 back up to my room. Grabbing my phone and Lunchable, I see there's an email from Mrs. Truss. Pulling down the notification bar, the email says that we still have to present our lab findings, and we're gonna do it tomorrow. On Zoom.

I have to see Kamron's face again.

Chapter Sixteen

My finger hovers over the Join Meeting button. It's ten minutes until class starts. I'm under my blankets in bed with a heating pad over my stomach because my period decided to show up last night. I sip my cup of ginger tea and click the button. The steam fogs up my blue light blocking glasses. In ten short minutes, I'm going to see Kamron's face. We already planned to take turns presenting. I can just go ahead and go first and then we go from there. I don't even have to talk to him.

Mrs. Truss lets us into the meeting room five minutes before class officially starts. My camera and mic are off. There's four of us in the virtual room. Brittney, Charlie, and Kamron are all in well-lit rooms looking at the screen. Of course Kamron is already here.

"Naima, I need you to turn on your video," Mrs. Truss tells me.

I snatch my head scarf off, quickly fluff my hair, and turn on the lamp on my nightstand. When I turn on the camera, Mrs.

Truss looks closer at her screen.

"Are you in bed, Naima? Is everything okay?"

This is why my camera was off. I unmute my mic.

"I'm just feeling a little bit under the weather." I fake a smile and push the bridge of my glasses upward.

Her mouth turns downward in a fake sympathetic smile. "I hope y'all are staying safe. Covid is really nasty right now."

I tighten my lips and avert my gaze. It's ridiculous that over half the people in this chat right now have a period, but if I say "I'm on my period," I've committed a social travesty because girls are just supposed to deal with this thing that disrupts our lives, and if we ask for a day off, it's asking for too much.

I take another sip of my tea as the rest of class slowly trickles in until it's time to start our presentations.

"Unless anyone wants to volunteer to go first," Mrs. Truss says. "We can go in the order that you sent them in. So it's Jess and Charlie, first. Kamron and Naima, second. Emma and Olivia, third. Maddie and Abbie, fourth. And Brittney and Dustin, last. Okay?"

Everyone nods on the screen.

"I'll share the PowerPoints on my end. Jess and Charlie, whenever you're ready."

A red number shows up on my chat box. A direct message. I click it.

KAMRON BARKSDALE (he/him): Do you want to go first or do you want me?

NAIMA GRACE: You go first

Kamron shifts in his little square but then stares directly at the camera. Almost like he's looking at me, but that's silly. He could be looking at anyone. While Jess and Charlie are presenting, I notice my hair is flat on one side. I tilt my head and play with my hair, slowly fluffing it out so it won't look flat when it's time to present. I sip my tea, and another direct message pops up.

KAMRON BARKSDALE (he/him): Your hair looks fine.

A smile creeps across my face, but when I realize what's happening, I gulp, put the mug down, and slide my glasses back up my nose. When I glance at the screen again, there's a smirk on his face. When he said "fine" did he mean it like "It looks alright so quit playing with it" or "It looks good and so do you?" My chest flutters because why would he think that? I kinda hope he thinks that.

No, he doesn't like you, Naima. He likes Kennedy.

I bite my lip, and my eyes scan the border of my laptop to avoid looking directly at the screen. Jess and Charlie wind down their presentation so that means that we're about to start. I open the Google Doc of our written presentation and use that as a script for when we start. Mrs. Truss pulls up our presentation, and Kamron's face lights up before going into the abstract. His voice deepens, and he speaks slower making sure the point gets across. Mrs. Truss clicks the next slide, and

I black out.

I know I have to talk about elodea. I go back and forth from the Google Doc to the screen and hope and pray whatever I'm saying makes sense. When I take a breath, Mrs. Truss clicks the next slide, and Kamron talks about our method and materials. Since there are two results slides. I go over the results from the first experiment. This time I've slowed down when speaking, getting more in the groove of the presentation. Kamron talks about our hypothesis and second experiment. I talk through the first part of the discussion, and Kamron follows up the second part and then goes into the conclusion.

"Good work, you two," Mrs. Truss says. "Emma and Olivia?"

I mute my mic and let out a huge exhale. Another direct message pops up.

KAMRON BARKSDALE (he/him): Good job, partner

I smile then cover my mouth with my hand. I survived my first big lab project with Kamron Barksdale.

⸺ 𝑒𝑙𝑒 ⸺

Let's review the facts, shall we?

FACT: Kamron says that we're friends.

FACT: Kamron added me to his close friends

FACT: Kamron said he wanted nothing else to do with Kennedy.

FACT: I kissed Kamron.

FACT: After that, he said he's sorry that he hurt me with Kennedy.

FACT: Yesterday during the presentation, Kamron direct messaged me that I looked nice and did a good job.

It doesn't make sense. Why would he say he won't speak to her and then the next day say he's hurt me because of her? How did he hurt me? When? The questions circle around my chest and stuff themselves in my throat. I cough—loosening them—and stretch my neck.

I need to ask, but how can I get to the bottom of it without him thinking I'm a creeper? I can't outright say, "Are you dating Kennedy?" because then he'll be like "Yes I am," and I don't want to hear that, or he'll be like, "No, I'm not and why are you so invested in my personal life?" and he'll probably never speak to me. So I have to be careful about what I say. I have to find a way around the question so I can get my answer, and he won't hate me.

What happens if I fail? Well first, Kamron could outright reject me. I'd lose my lab partner and may have to be paired with some other person in class. Or Mrs. Truss may not separate us, and the energy between us would be thick and impenetrable (i.e unbearable for me). It would wreck my grade, and I would fail in life.

The other and possibly worst option is that I lose the first friend I've made since Luna moved here when she was ten.

And Kamron is smart and kind, a little bit cocky, but he's refreshing. He's really easy to talk to. I got to talk about Dad, and I haven't done that with someone else since Mom got me a therapist after Dad's death. If Kamron isn't my friend, I'd lose all of that.

There's a knock on my bedroom door. It's Luna, waving two plastic bags in the air. "Our dresses are here!" she squeals.

It's early afternoon, but I'm stewing under my blankets in the dark. I turn on my lamp so she can see me. She sits besides me and plops the bags down at the foot of the bed.

"You still in bed, girl?" she asks.

"Just thinking about something," I say and then explain. "Yesterday during our presentation, Kamron was really nice to me, and I don't know—"

"Naima, don't do it. You were crying over that boy."

"I know, but maybe I was wrong. Maybe I misunderstood his text." That text and his actions don't line up. Something's off.

Luna sighs, clearly annoyed that I want to pursue it—and I will—with or without her support. I need to know the truth.

"What are you trying to text him?"

"I just want to know what he meant about Kennedy. Should I just say that? 'What did you mean about Kennedy?'"

She shrugs and leans to grab one of the plastic bags. "Sure."

I pull up his text and message him. I consider that I haven't texted him in five days, and it may be weird that I'm bringing this up now, but I don't care. I need to know.

As soon as I hit send, I flip the phone over so I can't see his reply.

"Let's try on these dresses!" I say to get my mind off the very risky text I just sent.

I tear the end of the plastic bag and pull the dress out. It's royal blue and shimmers. I fan it out and hold it up to gaze at it before getting out of bed and trying it on. It goes easily over my head. Looking in the mirror, it cloaks my frame the way I prefer my dresses to. From the mirror, I can see Luna behind me struggling to slip hers on. Her dress is bunched up around her chest. I turn around and attempt to push it down, but it won't budge.

"Maybe we should've ordered the same size." I let go of the dress when I realize it won't slide down her body.

"It's fine. I can make it fit." She keeps struggling to squeeze the dress over her shapewear. It's a little over a week until the dance. There's no time to send it back and get a new one.

"Do you want to switch?" I offer. I don't like super tight dresses, but my hips aren't as wide as Luna's. Maybe I could fit the dress easier.

She pulls the dress off of her and hands it to me. "Let's see."

I take off the blue dress and hand it to her. When I slide on the silver one, it slides on easier, but I have to shimmy around my hips. I check myself out in the mirror, and my tummy is more pronounced in this dress.

"Naima!" Luna walks around to look at the front of the dress. "You look hot."

I reflexively cover my midsection and grimace. "Really?"

"Definitely. Look at you!" She points to my reflection in the mirror. Her dress fits like a glove, hugging all of her curves.

"You look hot, too."

"I know." She tilts her head causing her loose bun to bop around. "So what are we thinking? Hair? Makeup?"

"Well, I like the makeup you showed me. I think that works better with this dress, especially with the highlights." The golds will pop against her skin tone and the dark blue dress. "What about me?"

She puts a finger on her lips to think and gazes at my hair and face. "I'm thinking nude makeup."

"How much blush?" I ask. Blush is my favorite part.

"I think your amount of blush will work," she laughs. "But I like your regular hair. Maybe add some clips or something. Ooooh, I've seen people put butterflies in their curls. How about that but stars?"

I look in the mirror and envision stars in my hair. Although cute, I think it'd be a nightmare to take down.

"We'll see," I tell her.

"That means no," she says. "Are you still going with Sam?"

Sam said he wanted to coordinate his suit with our dresses, but I never really asked him if he wanted to be a part of our group.

"I don't know. You wanna walk over and ask?"

We change out of our dresses and back into our clothes. I hang the silver dress up in the closet and check my phone. Kamron texted back.

KAMRON: She has covid

I show Luna the text, and her eyes widen. What does Kennedy having Covid have to do with anything? I look back at his texts where he talks about not wanting to hurt me because of Kennedy, but Kennedy has Covid? Did he have Covid? Is that what's wrong? As I'm processing it, another text slips through.

KAMRON: I've been testing everyday. I'm still negative, but I talked to her Thursday morning and then we worked on the project that night. She didn't tell me she had covid until after I left your house

Luna looks at the text and then me. "He thought he gave you Covid? Oh."

Oh is right. My meltdown over the weekend seems a bit more embarrassing now.

NAIMA: I don't have Covid. I've been testing negative, too

KAMRON: You were sick yesterday on zoom

NAIMA: My period

I send the text, and then realize that maybe talking about my period to a teenage boy is crass, but he has a sister and a mother. He'll get over it.

KAMRON: Oh

We have a lot of those going around.

NAIMA: I'm glad we cleared that up

KAMRON: Sorry to put you through that

Our texts send within moments of each other. I don't know how else to respond so I don't. I slide the phone in my jogger pockets. "Ready to go see Sam?"

Sliding on my Crocs, we walk across the yard to Sam's house. It's just his Jeep in the yard so Ms. Tish is at work. I knock twice before opening the screen door.

"It's me," I yell and walk towards his room where he's laying on his bed with his phone. He sits up when he sees me and Luna. "Hey. I wanted to ask you something?"

"What's up?" he says. Luna and I sit on opposite sides of him.

"Do you have a date for Homecoming?"

He narrows his eyes. "I thought I was going with y'all."

"What happened to that girl at the ice cream place?"

"That was...nothing."

"Sam!" Luna slaps his arm. "Why didn't you tell me you were dating again?"

He rubs his arm like Luna really hurt him. "I'm not dating again. It was one date."

We drop it although I really want to make fun of the fact that Sam is not a hot boy anymore. It's the middle of September, and this boy has been on like two dates the entire year? Some people peak in high school, so I figure I won't add salt to the wound.

"Guess who got Covid and shut down the whole school?" I ask him, my eyes gleaming with gossip.

He looks from me to Luna clueless.

"Kennedy," Luna says.

"No." He shakes his head in disbelief.

"Yes," I tell him. My beautiful perfect cousin is why we have to stay home for two weeks.

"You know Kennedy was always my favorite." He grins.

I shove his shoulder. "Shut up. She's not. You're just saying that cause you get to stay home and smoke weed."

"There's nothing else to do. Unless you want to throw the ball with me."

"God, no," I groan. Every year to warm up, Sam wants a buddy to help him get back in baseball shape. I don't know why he won't use Markese who's actually athletic; instead, he uses me. And I don't know how to catch or throw a ball so I'm literally the worst person to play catch with.

I rack my brain thinking of something besides baseball we can do because it's only Day 3 of our quarantine, and I am also bored. Usually, during the summer we plan to go to other towns where there's more stuff open, but he's right. We're done with school by noon, and nothing fun is open for miles. There's really nothing to do.

"Sam?" I ask, and he turns his attention to me. "Will you

teach me how to drive?"

Yes, driving terrifies me because it can kill me, but also Mom is right. It's a skill that would be so useful to me. Everyone my age can drive, even Luna who doesn't have her own car. Maybe it's about time I learn.

"You sure you're ready for that?" Sam asks.

I nod.

His lips slowly turn into a grin. "Okay, but you can't wreck my truck."

"I'm gonna ram it into a tree," I joke.

Chapter Seventeen

My hands grip the wheel at ten and two. There's a slight vibration from the wheel. I stare at the trees looking towards my house. I can do this. I know I can. I breathe deeply. In for four seconds and out for seven hoping that it'll assuage the pressure building up in my chest. In for four and out for seven.

"You can back up whenever you're ready," Sam says. He's holding onto the handle bar on the ceiling. We've been sitting here for at least ten minutes.

I close my eyes, breathe again, and remind myself that I can do this. I press the brakes and switch the gear to reverse. The Jeep jerks slightly, but it doesn't move. I lift my foot a centimeter, but it feels too sudden when it starts to move back, I slam the brakes. Sam grips the handle bar tighter.

"Okay. Just *slowly* take your foot off the brakes." He nods at me to show it's safe to follow his directions.

I ease off the brakes, and the car inches back.

"Just like that," he says. "And check your mirrors to make

sure you're not gonna hit anything."

I look out the side mirror and see a tree, ditch, and gravel road. I try to look in the rearview mirror, but it's too high. I have to sit up to even see out of it. I slam the brakes to readjust it. Sam steadies himself on the glove compartment. A tightness forms around my throat because I keep messing up. I try to breathe through it.

"You don't have to keep slamming the brakes. Just gently press it when you want to stop. Okay?"

I inhale. "Okay," I exhale.

"Let's try again."

I readjust my hands to ten and two, breathe, and then ease up off the brake. We're getting closer to the end of the driveway and on the gravel road.

"Okay now turn left."

I turn the wheel.

"That's your right, Nai."

I turn the wheel the other way where the car starts lining up with the driveway.

"Okay *gently* press the brakes," Sam instructs.

I press down on the brakes, and this time it doesn't send Sam flying towards the windshield.

"You're gonna put it in drive and then just go back and park."

I exhale. I can do this.

I turn the knob to Drive and ease my foot on the gas pedal.

It jolts, moving a little faster than I want it too so I slam down, thinking it's the brakes, but it's the gas. The car speeds across the driveway so I take my hands off the wheel, and my feet off the pedals to get it to stop.

"Brakes! Brakes! Brakes!" Sam yells.

My chest vibrates as I scream and wave my hands in the air trying to remember where the brakes are. My foot finds it and pushes it. The Jeep jerks again. Sam puts the truck in Park, presses the off button, and unbuckles his seat belt.

"We're done for today."

He grabs the fob, opens his door, and slams it shut. I lay my head against the wheel. I can't believe I did that. I could've hit a tree or something. Maybe I'm not as ready as I thought.

I sigh and lift my head up from the wheel. Sam's back is leaning against the side of the Jeep. When he sees me, he walks to the door and opens it.

"Come on," he says.

I slide out of the Jeep and watch the corner of his mouth lifts into a sympathetic smile. "We can try again tomorrow."

"I'm sorry." I avert my gaze and wrap my arms around my body.

"It's okay. Tomorrow, we're doing the basics. No driving for you until you learn your left from your right." He jokes and closes the door behind me.

"Okay, but that's really hard." Left and right makes no sense because they shift whenever you move whereas cardinal directions are static.

"It's really not. Come here." He wraps his arms around me and pulls me in for a bear hug. I lay against his chest, close my eyes, and breathe in the scent of fabric softener. His knuckles drag along my spine, releasing the tension in my back and chest. I inhale and exhale deeply before Sam pulls away from me.

"Feel better?"

I nod. I feel much better now.

The next day, we sit in the car. Sam tells me that the first thing I should do is adjust my mirrors. I fix the rearview mirror so I can see out the back window just by slightly turning my head. Then he makes me shift to each gear. Once I do that, he shows me how to turn on the lights and flash my bright lights. Finishing all that, he has me adjust the seat so I can be in a comfortable position. I realize that it's easier to reach the wheel when the seat is closer to it, and I lower the steering wheel so it's facing my chest instead of up towards my head. My hands feel more certain at ten and two now.

"We're gonna do this every time you get in. Okay?"

I nod. He leans back against his seat. "Welp, that's all for today."

"That's it?" I ask. We didn't even move the Jeep.

"Maybe we can try again this weekend, but you need to take

it *really* slow."

My head sinks causing my chin to touch my chest. Sam learned how to drive in a month. Luna learned in three. I thought this was just a thing that you get behind the wheel and go. You just drive. Sam's making it seem like I'm gonna need a lot more than three months to get there.

We get out of the car and go back to his room. Sam lays on the bed, and I sit at the foot of it. He scrolls on his phone while I pick at my fingernail. It's a little after two on a Friday. I try to see Dad on Fridays, but the stress of driving means my energy is spent. I don't like the idea of taking a super long time to learn this skill. I want a win.

"I'm thinking about dressing up next week for Spirit Week," I tell Sam.

"Why?" he asks. The phone still covers his face.

"I don't know. It's fun and there's nothing else to do."

"But no one's going to see it."

"I'll post on social media. Do you want to dress up with me?"

Now he moves the phone out of his face to look at me. "Are the days boring or are there any good ones?"

I bite my lip. "I don't know. I'll look."

I grab my phone from his desk and search the school's website. I have to scroll past the Covid outbreak memo to get to the original Spirit Week post.

"Okay Monday is Decades Day. We dress up as our favorite

decade. Tuesday is Teen Beach Day. Dress up as a biker or a surfer. Wednesday is Wacky Wonderland so tacky day. Thursday is Tweedledee & Tweedledum so we can be twinsies, and Friday is Spirit Day."

"I like the decades and twins," he says before returning to his phone.

"So you'll dress up with me?" A grin spreads across my face.

"Sure."

I clap my hands and squeal. Decades day and Twinsies Day. "Which decade do you want to do?"

He squints his eyes and puckers his lips. "I don't know. The eighties seems fun and kinda easy."

"I feel like Mom has stuff from back in the day, like the 90s and 2000."

"We can do that," Sam agrees so I wiggle in place.

***

Sam and I are in the extra bedroom sifting through storage boxes. Friday, most of our teachers gave us the next week's assignments so I did them over the weekend and turned them in this morning. Thank God there are no Zooms this week so I'm free to dress up for Spirit Week and have the scariest driving lessons with Sam.

From my research, I saw that early 2000s fashion consisted of a lot of track suits and flat bellies. They didn't have a lot of examples of what that fashion looked like on fat girls. The ones I could find looked like church ladies so I'm improvising. Sam pulls out storage boxes and we look through them. Most are lower-level holiday and birthday decorations. We keep the Christmas ones in the garage. He grabs another box, and it's filled with my childhood awards and drawings. I make a note to look at it later because if I do it now, I'll forget to dress up. There's another box with Markese's stuff. Under all of those storage boxes are two boxes filled with clothes.

"I think this is it." I sit on a storage box and slide the other box towards me. Sam sits beside me.

When Dad died, Mom donated most of his clothes, but she kept his favorites. At the top of the box is his Alcorn sweater. Mom and Dad didn't meet in college actually. Mom went to Mississippi State. They met afterwards when Dad signed up for the Teacher Loan Forgiveness Program. He came back home to Redbud Springs to teach, and this school district was one of two places where Mom found a job after college.

I missed when they would tell the story. Dad said he was so nervous talking to Mom because she was brilliant and beautiful. And Mom said she thought Dad was eclectic but adorable. He always did a cute little wave whenever he saw her. His arm would be tucked into his side, and he'd wave near his chest. He would still do it when he was nervous but wanted to be polite.

I rub the purple and gold stitching on the sweatshirt.

"You okay?" Sam asks. He leans towards me and rubs my

back.

"Yeah, I was just thinking about Dad." His lips draw into a line like *we can pack up if this is too painful for me*, but I reassure him, "It was a good memory."

I place the sweater to the side. We dig through, and there's a number of graphic tees and a few pairs of jeans. Sam slides the other box over, and there's a few more of Dad's stuff but more of Mom's. I find a cute denim mini dress. I grab it and pull the fabric to see if it gives. It does slightly.

"I'm trying it on." I walk behind Sam and turn around so he can't see my body while I change out of my pajamas and into the dress. When I unzip it, it comes up to my chest, but I can't reach the zipper.

"Help."

He jumps up from the box and tries to zip it, but it's stuck. I suck in my belly and nothing.

"Mom wasn't lying when she said she used to be skinny," I sigh and sit back down on the box in the unzipped dress. Sam sits besides me and goes through the box with Dad's clothes. Mom has mini skirts and bikini tops and towards the bottom there's an oversized red bandana with straps on it. I pick it up and stretch it out. It's spandex!

"Okay, I'm wearing this!" I tell Sam. He's on his phone, but he looks up to see the top. He swallows, and I know he wants to say something smart. "I'm gonna look cute."

"Sure." He rolls his eyes, but then shows me the phone.

There are five white boys with different graphic tees, spiky hair, jeans, and blazers. "I'm thinking of maybe doing jeans, one of these tee shirts, and your dad's letterman jacket."

"What about the spiky hair?" I grin.

"No." He shakes his head.

"Come on. You don't want to bleach the ends? It'll be fun." I bump his shoulder with mine.

He puts his finger up. "Maybe a bandana. Do you have a red one? We could match."

"Yeah, it's probably upstairs."

We grab the clothes we want to wear and stack the other boxes back against the wall. He follows me up to my room, and I search my top drawer where there's a red bandana near the back that I haven't worn in a while. I hand it to him and shoo him out of my room so I can change. Sitting on my bed, I google "bandana shirt 2000s" and see a picture of Beyoncé. I look at the top in my hands and realize it's the same top. Not Mom tryna be a baby Beyoncé.

In the picture, Beyoncé is wearing low rise blue jeans, and her curly hair has golden clips on the side. I grab a pair of high waisted jeans from my dresser and change into the top and jeans. Then I search through my bobby pin container for gold clips and put them on either side of my hair. I step back from the mirror and admire how cute I look. I check myself out one more time before joining Sam downstairs whose standing in clothes so baggy they look like they're swallowing him. The red bandana is folded up and ties his curls back away from his face.

He opens his arms wide to display his outfit. "What do ya think?"

"I feel like I never see your forehead." It's kinda big. No wonder he covers it up with his curly bangs.

"I mean my outfit."

"Oh. It looks fine. You ready to take pictures?"

"Yeah," he answers.

We walk outside where there's better lighting. Sam's fiddling with his tripod while I stand with my legs twisted and swinging my arms so he knows where to set up the camera. When it's done, he comes and stands beside me.

"How do you want to take it?" he asks.

"I don't know. How did people pose back then?"

I grab my phone and Google "early 2000s poses." There are pics of girls with their hands on their hips. I cringe thinking about replicating that. I see a few guys holding up peace signs or holding both hands up with their three middle fingers down and their tongue hanging out. I show Sam, and he nods.

Sam presses the timer button, and I scrunch my face, holding my hands up with my thumbs and pinkies out and stick my tongue out. He widens his stance and balls his hands together in front of his chest. We practice doing it a few times before we look at the photos. I don't care what Sam wants so I delete the ones where my face looks funny or where I don't like the way

I look. There's three pics left to choose from.

"You can pick any you want." I hand the phone back to Sam after I sent the pics to myself. "Are you gonna post a photo of me?"

He snaps his fingers. "Why don't we take a video? Then I can put it on TikTok."

I roll my eyes. "I can't wait for the 'Who is your Black girlfriend?' comments."

"Okay, so don't be in this video."

"They do it every time, Sam. What's wrong with your fans?"

"They're not fans....They're followers."

"Yes, a cult following of people who are auditioning for the day that they can get in your pants."

"Naima!" he blushes.

"It's true! I find people attractive, but I'm not in their comments publicly thirsting over them. It's like have some dignity, ladies."

"It's not even like that."

I wag my finger at him when I finally figure out what it is. "You like the attention. You like having girls publicly adore you, you slut."

"And? It's nice to have people say nice things about me."

"I say nice things about you."

"When?" He tilts his head.

I scrunch my face trying to remember the last time I said something nice to him. I shift, glancing at the telephone pole at the end of the yard, racking my brain for a memory, any memory.

"Uh-huh." He nods his head triumphantly.

He's right. Maybe I haven't said nice things to him recently. I sit down on the porch and dangle my feet off the edge. He joins me.

"You have more to offer the world than your looks," I remind him.

He shrugs. "It doesn't hurt to be told that I look nice from time to time."

"Fine." I roll my eyes. "I guess the girls are right. You can be cute sometimes."

"Really?" He grins, and the laugh rolling up from my belly squeezes my eyes shut.

"Shut up. Everyone tells you you're cute."

"You're cute, too," he tells me.

"I know." I pucker my lips, and when his mouth widens, I grin. "But thank you."

Chapter Eighteen

When I wake up, I roll over and check my phone. Opening Instagram, I click the notification bar and see there are two likes on the picture of me and Sam that I posted to my story: Luna and Kamron. I sit up in bed and click on the story again, looking to see what Kamron may have seen and why he'd like it. There I am doing a silly rockstar face next to Sam. Did he think I was goofy or cringy or cute? Does Kamron liking my story means he likes me?

I dance with my hands before getting out of bed and going downstairs to make a bowl of cereal. Sitting at the kitchen table, I shove bites of Cinnamon Toast Crunch in my mouth with one hand and stare at the notification with my other. What does this mean?

I haven't talked to Kamron since our clarification last week. Now that I know he's definitely not with Kennedy, other questions seeped through. Like what did it mean when he held my hand in class? Or even when he got kicked out of class because I did? Did he really kiss me back or was I imagining that? I wonder what would've happened if Sam didn't bust in and ruin it.

I put the spoon down and tap my fingers against the table debating whether or not I should just message him. Maybe I'm mistaken or what if I'm right? What if Kamron likes me like Luna thought or what if we're really just friends? What if he's just being nice to me, and I'm reading too much into this? We haven't talked about the kiss since it happened, and I don't know if I should be grateful or terrified? What if it was a bad kiss? I've never kissed anybody on the lips before, and now I have a new fear.

My leg bounces on the stretcher of the chair as I exhale and stare at the phone. He's just my lab partner who liked a picture I took. It's a friendly like. That's it. That's all this is. If he likes me as a friend and only a friend that's no biggie. The sinking feeling in my tummy and tingle in my cheeks tells me that it is kind of a biggie. Why do I care so much about what Kamron thinks? Why do I want him to like me? A text pops up on my phone.

SAM: Im up whenever your ready to drive

Yesterday, I did pretty good at our driving lesson. We moved the car, and I didn't panic after hitting the gas pedal, so progress. I touch the message to reply.

NAIMA: Eating breakfast. Be over soon

I guzzle the cinnamon milk, put the bowl and spoon in the dishwasher, then head up to my room. Tuesday is Bikers or

Surfers day for Spirit Week. I don't have a motorcycle or a surfboard, but I figure I could wear a swimsuit. I grab my floral Torrid two piece swimsuit. The bottoms are high-waisted which makes me feel like I'm from the 1950s without actually being in the 1950s. Although I pulled out the padding from the top, it still makes me uncomfortable with how high my chest sits. I decide to grab the beach hat that I bought last summer when Sam drove us down to Pensacola. Looking in the mirror, I check out how adorable I am.

I grab a loose dress out of my closet and slip it on over the bathing suit. Then I grab my beach bag and stuff a striped towel in it before I head downstairs and walk over to Sam's. He's laying in his bed on his phone. Damp air from his shower wafts out of the bathroom while I'm standing in his doorway. I knock, and he sits up.

"Where are you going?"

"It's Spirit Week!" I remind him. "Can you take a picture of me?"

He pulls his phone in front of him and taps the screen.

"Outside." I roll my eyes and walk down the hallway to the front door. I look around his yard and decide to take the pictures in front of the dense wall of trees across from his front door. I run over the gravel driveway and turn around so he knows where to shoot. Staring at the phone, he follows me.

"I'm taking pictures," he says while I'm standing there waiting for him.

Gasping, I yank the dress off and swing the bag around to pose with it. I put my hand on my hat and tilt my head back to laugh. I kick one foot up behind me while I stand on the tippy toes of the other. Then I drop the bag in front of my stomach and look away from the camera. When I turn back towards the camera, I reach for the phone to see the pictures.

I delete half of them immediately because I don't like the face I'm making or the way my body looks. With the other half, I'm stunned at how great I look.

"You're such a good photographer," I tell Sam while still looking at the photos of me. I can't choose between four, so I send them to myself and decide to do a collage for my story. I hand his phone back to him and grab mine out of the beach bag to post on my story. I wonder if Kamron's going to like these. I smile and then tuck my phone away.

"You ready to drive?" I ask Sam.

We add onto yesterday's lesson. Today, Sam wants me to focus on backing up, pulling in, and parking. Although I'm still death gripping the wheel, I'm doing much better than I did the other day. My seat is adjusted to a comfortable position. The mirrors are adjusted to my height. I can do this, and I do! After an hour, I can now back a car up, pull into a space, and park a car. I'm getting pretty good at this thing.

When we finish, the first thing I do is open Instagram and sure enough, Kamron's there. He liked my story! I grin at my phone as I slide out of the Jeep's driver seat.

"You okay?" Sam chuckles. I probably look weird cheesing at my phone.

"Yeah," I say. I'm great actually.

Instead of hanging out at Sam's, I walk back home. When I get to my bed, I click Kamron's profile. He has an active story for close friends. Clicking on it, I see that the clay from last week is now a brown teapot that he's shaping. I reply to the story: *That looks really cool.*

I tuck my bottom lip inwards to nibble it when I press send. Hopefully, he doesn't think I'm being weird, but he did tell me that he did pottery, and he added me to his close friends. Those are the facts. Maybe it's okay that I'm messaging him.

A green dot shows up next to his profile pic. He's online! And then a text bubble shows up at the bottom of the Instagram chat. He's typing!

He replies: *Thanks. Been feeling inspired lately.*

Not sure how to respond to that, so I double tap his reply. It's only when I put my phone down that I realize, I've been smiling the whole time.

❧

"**D**o you think you're ready for the road?" Sam asks me. Yesterday, I mastered parking, now today we're pushing the limits.

"What are you thinking?" I ask. My hands are on the steering wheel at ten and two as I look ahead at the trees that divide Sam's yard from mine.

"Just up and down this road?" He points behind him to the dirt road. "We can go slow. No need to rush."

"Okay, so back up," he instructs, holding onto the grab handle. I back up slowly, barely lifting my foot off the brake.

"Turn around," he continues.

I turn the wheel and lightly press the gas. The Jeep jerks, but I take another breath and apply gentle pressure to the pedal. The Jeep creeps to the edge of the driveway.

"Which way?" I ask.

"Whichever way you want."

Knowing this road ends at Ms. Maybelle's, I turn toward the dead end and creep towards her house. The steering wheel jerks more from the gravel on the road, but I tighten my grip on the wheel. We make it to her house. Her driveway is a roundabout so I follow it to get back on the road.

"Okay," I exhale. "That wasn't that bad."

"Do you want to try and go to the other end of the road?" he asks.

"We can try." I nod nervously.

I take another deep breath before applying light pressure on the gas pedal and easing towards the highway. When we make it, Sam instructs me to do another turn. I do, slowly, and then wait for further instruction.

"Do you want to try it again? Maybe faster this time?" he

asks.

"I was going at a pretty reasonable speed."

"It said three miles per hour, Nai."

I exhale deeply. "Fine. How about five?"

"I think you can do ten."

I take another deep breath and release it. I tighten my grip on the steering wheel and then press down on the pedal. The Jeep jerks. Sam tightens his grip on the grab bar, and I apply slightly more pressure than I did before. I keep looking down at the speedometer, watching it slowly creep up. Five miles per hour. Six. Seven.

I glance from the speedometer to the road trying to see if I can get up to ten. When I look up again, I see antlers, then a deer's body five feet in front of the jeep, and then its tail as it makes its way to the other side of the road.

I slam the brakes. My grip tightens on the wheel. My heart pounds against my chest and eardrums. I open my mouth, but it feels like the words are closing in on themselves, choking me. I try to breathe again, but my body struggles to suck in air causing me to hyperventilate. My left arm tingles so I squeeze my hand to loosen it, but it doesn't help. Nothing does.

Sam turns the knob to Park, slings his door open, and rushes to the other side. He opens my door and unlatches my seat belt.

"Naima, are you okay?" he asks softly, cupping my face

Slowly, I shake my head. My breaths are still shallow and shaky. He rubs my back. "Breathe. Everything's alright."

I try to breathe, but my chest feels tighter like it's squeezing me. It's impossible.

"Breathe. Just breathe," Sam repeats as he rubs my back up and down my spine. Although it usually works, this time is different.

"I...think...I'm...dying," I tell him. Tears fill my eyes. This can't be the end of my life. I'm only sixteen.

He stares at me and nods. "Okay. What do you want to do?"

"Hospital?"

"Yeah. Come on." He reaches around my waist to gently help me out of the driver's seat and walk me over to the passenger seat. He buckles my seat belt for me before hopping back in the Jeep and taking off.

I'm watching the trees pass by and trying but failing to steady my breath. My chest is still painfully tight so I shift in the seat to try and help it, but I end up squirming.

"Lift your arms above your head," Sam says.

I do and some of the tightness eases up in my chest.

"Did it help? It helps with asthma."

I nod. I keep my arms elevated so I can take slower breaths, and it helps. We pull into the urgent care. Sam walks over to my side and helps me out. He loops his arm through mine as we walk in. I check in on the kiosk, and we sit in the back of the waiting room in front of the windows. I glance at the other people waiting: a mother with her young son in a wheelchair, an elderly woman with a cane, and a middle aged man with crutches.

I lay my head on Sam's shoulder and breathe deeply. He wraps his arm around me and rubs my arm. "Just keep breathing, okay? I'm here," he reassures me.

We wait for over an hour before my name is called. Sam walks with me to triage. The white nurse takes my vitals and does a double take at my hair. It's Wacky Wednesday so I'm wearing a tie dye shirt with black shorts over colorful leggings. My hair is in five puffs with different colored scrunchies. I'm a sight to see, I'm sure.

"It's Spirit Week," I explain.

They nod and ask about my symptoms so I tell them about the tingling in my arm, the tightness in my chest, and the trouble breathing.

"Do you have any comorbidities?" they ask.

I swallow, knowing this is when I say that I'm autistic, but even medical professionals are so ill-informed about autism that they'll think I'm incompetent and can't make my own decision.

"No." I hate lying, but I hate being infantilized more. I mean, technically, I'm not lying. Sure, autism can make experiences more intense for me, but I'm not tragically autistic. My existence isn't something I pathologize.

They input the rest of my info and tell me that because I'm sixteen, the doctor can see me, but without Sam since he's not family or an adult.

"I recommend you call your parents," they tell me before sending us back out to the waiting room.

"I'll text your mom," Sam says while we wait to be seen by the doctor. It's only 10:40 so Mom's still at school. Another thirty minutes pass before a nurse with bright red hair finally calls me back.

"I'll be right here," Sam tells me.

I walk into the tiny room, and she tells me that the doctor will be in shortly. While I wait, my eyes glance around the room to the jar of cotton balls, box of gloves, and medical waste bin on the counter. A Covid-19 graphic hangs on the wall. My feet swing back and forth as I nervously wait for an answer. After a few minutes, a middle-aged Black woman walks in.

"You're Naima?" she asks. I nod. "I'm Dr. Stevens. I'm just going to check your heart." She places her stethoscope on my back. "Can you take a deep breath for me?" I do and then she moves it to another spot on my back. "Again?" I breathe again and then she places it on my chest. "One more time." I breathe as she's listening.

She grabs the chair near the wall to sit closer to me and glances at the clipboard. "It says you're here because you're having trouble breathing and tightness in your chest. Can you explain what happened before you experienced this?"

"Yeah. I was driving and then a deer crossed the road, and my heart started beating fast, and my arm started tingling, and it felt like I was dying."

"Hmmm." Her eyebrows scrunch together. "Has anything like this happened before?"

I shake my head no.

"Well, your blood pressure is normal. Your pulse is slightly elevated, but your heart sound fine. It seems to me like you had a panic attack. You said this is your first time so I doubt it's an anxiety or panic disorder. My best advice is to go home and get some rest. If you keep having panic attacks, I would recommend you see a therapist. They can prescribe something if the problem is ongoing. Do you have any questions for me?"

I shake my head again. She smiles softly. "Take care of yourself. I hope you have a good rest of your day."

"You too," I say before she leaves the room. When I walk out, Mom is there with Sam.

"Naima!" She rushes to me with her arms wide open. "Sam told me everything. Are you okay?"

My eyes widen. "Aren't you supposed to be at work?"

"You're more important than work." She puts her hands on my shoulders. "What's going on?"

"The doctor said I had a panic attack," I tell them.

Mom squeezes me again and rubs my back. "I'm so sorry, Naima."

Sam rubs my arm and smiles sympathetically.

Mom wraps her arm around me. "I got it from here, Sam. Thank you for taking care of her."

I smile at him to say thank you as well.

"See y'all at home," he says.

With her arms cradled around me, Mom walks me to her truck. She presses the button to start it but grips the steering wheel and stares out in the parking lot. "This is all my fault, Naima."

"It's not your fault, Mom." She wasn't behind the wheel. She couldn't control the deer.

"It is." Her voice shakes. When she turns to look at me, her eyes are filled with tears.

"I push you entirely too hard. It's just, when Malcolm died, I worried—" Her head sinks. "I didn't think—I assumed he'd be here forever. That we'd raise you both until you're grown and when he died—" She turns back to the parking lot, and I watch a tear shimmer down her face. She wipes it away. "When he died, I worried about what y'all would do without me. If you'd be okay. We don't have anyone else."

After Dad died, and I was diagnosed, most of our family cut us off. They thought that autism could be caught by vaccines or close contact or that it could be prayed away. The vaccines excuse was ridiculous because we were all vaccinated as children, and I was the only autistic one. My paternal grandma thought it was just the devil that got ahold of me, and if I fought harder, I could get rid of it. Mom, in an effort to protect me, cut us off from them. So she's right. If she died, it'd just be me and Markese.

"I don't blame you, Naima. For them leaving. You're a child, but I wanted to prepare you for the day that I'm not there. I wanted to make sure that you can take care of yourself and your brother if you need to."

Her shoulder sinks. She looks up at the roof of the car and blinks away tears. Although Dad's been dead for two years, she's never really talked to me about what it was like for her to lose him. I only know what it's like to lose my father. I never imagined how hard it was for her and how she learned to cope with his absence.

But still, she's all I have, and all I ever wanted is for her to see me now, as I am. Not as I could be or who she imagined I am. I want her to make sure I am okay now instead of worrying about some future version of me that isn't promised to us.

"But you're here now. I need you now," I say.

When she turns to look at me, her eyes are red-rimmed and puffy. I return her gaze. I want her to know how desperately I need her to see me and accept me as I am with all of my imperfections and limitations. I need her to hold me and love me forever. To just be my Mom, not someone I have to hide from or perform for.

Tears well in my eyes to mirror hers. As one slides down my cheek, she wipes it away with her thumb.

"I'm sorry," she says.

I reach over the console and hug her. She squeezes me back. We hold each other with the realization that we need each other to survive this. When her back pats slow, I realize that

I'm still squeezing her. I release my hold on her and sit up. We wipe our eyes and sniffle.

"Whew, I needed that," she says, returning her hands to ten and two on the wheel. She turns over to me and smiles. "Do you want McDonald's?"

"Can I get a Happy Meal?" I ask.

She laughs. "Of course you can, baby."

Chapter Nineteen

It's hard having a panic attack and not feeling broken in some way. Like this is not the way my body is supposed to work, but here I am causing this malfunction. After the hospital, I took a nap and slept fine that night. Mom took today off of work to stay home with me. She's downstairs while I'm in my room rewatching *She-Ra and the Princesses of Power*.

The deer made me realize how much I'm still affected by Dad's death. I was trying to be a normal teenager who learned how to drive, but that's kind of hard when I lack coordination and when driving—although a normal skill and a prerequisite for society—can be deadly. Maybe Sam was right when he said I needed to take it slow. I was just so offended and thought that maybe he was calling me slow, and I had to prove to him that I wasn't. I'm always fighting instead of accepting that I have limitations, but it's just hard seeing everyone else around me pick up something so easily while I struggle with it.

And Mom. I just assumed that Mom would tell me to be

better in school because she was embarrassed by having an autistic child. I didn't realize that it was because she was afraid of what would happen to us if she died. I don't want to think about that even though I know it's inevitable. I wish she would've told me instead of me assuming the worst of her. Instead of me assuming that she hates me.

My phone lights up with a text from Sam asking to come over. I haven't seen him since yesterday at the hospital. I'm guessing he left me alone to rest. After a few minutes, I hear the knock on the door and the slow drag of his feet against the hardwood floor and then up the stairs.

"Hey," he says standing in the doorway. "Feeling better?"

I nod and smile at him. He walks in and sits at the foot of my bed.

"Thank you." I smile weakly. "For taking care of me yesterday."

"Of course." He squeezes my foot.

I scoot over, flip up the covers on that side of the bed, and pat the empty space for him to join.

"Shoes," I remind him.

He slides them off and joins me. I lay the covers on top of him. With his arm wrapped around my shoulders, I lean over on his chest and relax into the scent of fresh laundry. His hand rubs the side of my arm, and my eyes grow heavy from the sensation and the whistling of his hand moving back and forth. I exhale forcefully and close my eyes because it's easier.

"I um—" I clear my throat. "I guess this means driving lessons are over."

"If you want them to be." His voice is soft, and he goes from rubbing my arms with his palms to just his fingertips.

"I still have to learn how to drive, but I think you're right. We have to go really slow." My heart tightens. As much as I want to fight it, it's the truth. Some things I'm better at than my peers and others I'm worse at. Driving is gonna take me a lot longer than it took him.

"We can go as slow as you need to."

"It still makes me feel like a failure," I admit.

"Nai, you're great at everything," he scoffs. "You're damn near perfect. I'm only good at one thing, and it's driving."

I lift up from his chest and open my eyes. "Didn't you call me mean and say that I need to compliment you more? You don't compliment yourself."

"What are you talking about?"

"You're great at a lot of things." I point at my index finger to start counting. "One, TikTok. You have two *million* followers. Two, you can be friends with anybody. Three, you're great at sports. Four, you've saved my life more times than I can count. Five—"

He puts his hand on top of mine to get me to stop counting. "I get it. I'm amazing." He rolls his eyes but grins widely, his attempt at a humble brag.

"You *are* amazing. I just froze yesterday, and you knew exactly what to do. I couldn't even think or move. It was terrifying. I don't know what I would've done without you."

Tears well in my eyes. If I had to face that alone, who knows how long I'd be in that car or even if I would've survived. A panic attack feels one step away from a heart attack or death.

He offers a soft smile and wipes the tear from my cheek.

"I'm sorry," I say. "If I ever made you feel bad about anything I said. I'm just playing with you. I don't ever want to offend you, but I realize that sometimes I cross the line, and if I ever hurt you, I'm sorry. You don't deserve that."

He reaches for my hand and squeezes it. "This is why I tell you you're not funny."

I playfully slap his arm, and he laughs. "No, but thank you for that. I appreciate it."

I wrap my arms around his shoulder and kiss his temple. "You're my best friend, and I love you."

He looks at me, his hazel eyes warm and soft when he smiles. "I love you, too."

I lay my head on his shoulder, and he kisses the top of it. "Does this mean I'm a better friend than Luna?" he asks.

"Oh, you can never compare to Luna." I grin.

He scoffs.

"Luna's a perfect angel that fell from the sky, and you're you."

He drops his shoulder so my head falls. "What happened to being nice to me?"

"I'm just saying I can see myself buying a house with Luna and raising babies together. I can't imagine a world without her in it." I place my hand over my heart. Imagine spending the rest of your life with your best friend. It's a dream come true.

"So you want to be a lesbian?"

"I doubt I'm even Luna's type. You can live with someone and raise babies with them platonically."

"I'm just saying you're my best friend so it would—"

"Wait," I interrupt him. "I'm at the top?" Like the tippy top? I know Luna considers me her top best friend because she's my top best friend, but do two people think of me as their bestest best friend?

"Between Darius, Marcus, and Jeff? Yeah."

"Jeff?"

He rolls his eyes. "You do this every time. Jeff, blond hair, blue eyes? We play baseball together."

"The white one you're always with?" I keep forgetting about him. He doesn't have a spicy name that dances on the tongue like Darius or Marcus or Luna or Naima. It's just Jeff. Boring.

"Yeah."

"Okay but who names their kid, Jeff?"

"My name is Samuel. It's not that different."

"Yeah, but I've known you for how long?" I blink to do the math. "Eleven years?"

"Damn," he chuckles. "Eleven years?"

I stare into his hazel eyes and remember the bright eyed little boy that I met eleven years ago. The boy that's grown up beside me, held my hand, and comforted me for all of these years. The boy that I can't really imagine a life without. Eleven years is most of our lifetime, and I'm a good enough friend that he *wanted* to spend it with me.

Maybe everyone was right. I am too much, too loud, too weird. For them. But for Luna and Sam, I am just right. I'm more than alright. I'm the best. Just by being me.

Sam stays with me for a couple more hours to watch *She-Ra*. When he says he's going home, I walk him downstairs and sit at the bar while Mom's in the kitchen leaning over the counter on her phone.

"You hungry?" she asks, and I nod.

She turns around to open the fridge. "Peanut butter and jelly, okay?" she asks.

"That's fine."

She grabs the jelly from the fridge and pulls out the bread and peanut butter from the pantry. I watch her as she twists the tops off and slides the peanut butter then jelly onto the bread. My mouth twitches. There's this awkward space between us. A limbo. Even though we cried in the car yesterday, and I told her how I feel, I know there's more left unsaid. I feel it.

"Toasted?" she asks. She knows I love the way the peanut butter gets gooey and the bread gets crunchy when it's toasted.

"Please." I smile.

She returns my smile before sticking the sandwich in a slot

and pulling the lever down. She leans against the sink and stands at the toaster with her hands folded. We wait. I gaze at my thumb nail while I scratch it with my finger. The sandwich pops up, and she grabs a paper towel to place it on. Pulling the drawer out, she grabs a knife to cut it diagonally and slides the paper towel over to me.

"Capri sun?" she asks.

I nod with the sandwich halfway to my mouth. I bite into it and the warm peanut butter and jelly smooths over my tongue. She grabs the Capri Sun from the fridge, lays it on the bar, then props her elbows on the counter to gaze at me. Her mouth opens, like she wants to say something, but then she closes it. I swallow the bite of sandwich and take another, not knowing what to say to make Mom quit hovering and staring at me.

"Good?" Mom asks, and I nod. Grabbing the straw on the Capri Sun, I poke a hole in the pouch and bring it to my lips, not taking my eyes off of Mom. She sighs.

"I'm really sorry, Naima." Her gaze is unwavering even as tears fill the corner. She steeples her fingers over her mouth. I open my mouth to protest her apology, but she puts her hand up to stop me. "I should've listened to you, and I didn't. You said you were trying your best, and I should've taken your word for it. I should've always sided with you. I'm sorry."

Her hands clasp in front of her. A plea. I blink away the apology because it's not what I really want.

"Why didn't you tell me?"

"What?" she blinks.

"About Dad. How hard it was for you?"

For so long there was nowhere for my grief to go, and no one to share it with. I thought I was alone. I thought I was the only one working so hard to keep Dad's memory alive, that I was the only one hurting because he wasn't here anymore. His boisterous laugh. His silly grin. How he would open his arms wide, as far as they'd go, and say, "I love you this much," and when I run to him, he'd wrap his arms around me in a hug.

Mom leans on the counter, eyeing me, debating how much she wants to share. "Our grief was not the same. I lost my husband, but you lost your father, and you were young." She pauses. "It wasn't fair to burden you with what I was going through."

I draw my hands together and place my head on them while I process her words.

"I needed to talk about him with someone other than Dr. Carpenter," I tell her. "It's like when I talk about him, he's still here with us, and when you'd get mad at me after he died...I felt...I thought...you hated me."

She scurries around the counter to the bar and cups my face. "Naima, no. I could never hate you, baby." She draws my head into her chest and rubs my back. "You are perfect, Naima."

The tension in my shoulders releases when I lay my head against her heart. She pulls me away, her hands lightly press into my cheeks as she stares into my eyes. My chest heaves under the intensity of her gaze, but she wants me to know that she's telling the truth. I nod, and she returns my nod and then sits in the chair beside me. She swivels her seat around until our knees touch and places her hand on my knee.

"When Sam got mad at you a few weeks ago. I got nervous. I trust him. I do"—she's quick to add—"but if he can drop you like that. I wanted you to be able to take care of yourself. I still do." Her hands find mine and hold it. "I hope you can forgive me."

I stare at her hands as they hold mine. I was never really mad at Mom, just hurt. Just searching for some solace, some respite in my grief. That was all I really wanted.

"Will you be transparent with me from now on? About your why? I think I'm old enough to know."

She sighs then chews on her bottom lip. She nods. "I can do that." She pats my knee as she gets up from her seat and walks back around to the other side of the counter.

"Are you any better since yesterday?" she asks once she's facing me again.

I nod. "Having Sam over helped."

"He's a good friend," she says.

"I told him that."

"And what about Kamron? He hasn't been over in a while. Is everything okay with your project?" She opens the fridge door and pulls out the pitcher of sweet tea.

"Yeah, we finished the lab last week. Got an A. He probably

won't be over again until we start our new lab next quarter."

"You sure about that?" she asks leaning back against the sink to pour herself a cup of tea.

My eyebrows furrow while I decipher what she means.

"You want me to be transparent?" She sits the cup down and puts the pitcher back in the fridge before turning to me. "He likes you."

I shake my head. "He doesn't." That's not a fact. All I know is that we're friends. Also when I asked for transparency, it was about parenting intentions, not boys.

A grin creeps across her face as she brings the sweet tea to her lips. "Okay. I'm just saying boys don't douse themselves in that much cologne unless they're trying to make a good impression."

"You smelled that?"

"They could smell him all the way to town. Listen, I see it all the time in the classroom. Someone's got a crush."

The prickly feeling returns to my cheeks.

"Um-hmm." She laughs and squeezes my shoulder to walk past me to go to her room.

First Luna and now Mom. Am I really being oblivious? Is it really as simple as he likes me, and I'm complicating things by thinking someone like him would never like someone like me? That we could only ever be friends? I lay my head against the cool tile of the bar. I guess I'll find out next week when school reopens.

I don't have to wait till next week because Kamron texts me around eight at night.

KAMRON: I guess Twiddledee and Twiddledum was too hard

NAIMA: What?

KAMRON: spirit week

I gasp. Of course. I completely forgot about Spirit Week and that me and Sam were supposed to dress up today as twins. I tap the screen not sure what to send back when he sends another message.

KAMRON: everything ok?

I've done so much talking today that I should be exhausted. Maybe I shouldn't go into this with Kamron. Two months ago I didn't even know the guy, but every time I talk to him, he just gets it. He understands. So I tell him the truth.

NAIMA: No. I had a panic attack.

I gnaw on my lip. Even though he doesn't seem like the type that would stigmatize mental health problems, I don't know. This is a risk.

KAMRON: oh shit you been resting and taking care of yourself?

NAIMA: Yeah

KAMRON: you wanna talk about it?

I exhale. Do I wanna talk about it? I've been talking all day, but I guess with Sam and Mom, I've been talking around it. Do I actually want to talk about everything?

NAIMA: Sure

KAMRON: Okay I'll call you.

Call? I panic then realize that maybe I don't actually need to talk. His name pops up at the top of my screen, and I muster all the courage I have to answer it.

"Hello?" I say then scrunch my face. I probably sound so awkward, and he hates the sound of my voice.

"Naima? Hey." I can hear the smile in his voice, and my heart thumps against my chest in response. It's been weeks since I've heard the breathless way he says my name.

"Hey. You wanted...to...talk?" I squeeze my eyes shut. *Please, quit being awkward, Naima.*

"Yeah, is this okay? I felt like it'd be easier than typing everything out."

"Yeah that makes sense. I just—"

"Does it make you nervous?"

"A little, yeah." I bite my bottom lip. I don't want him to not talk to me, but this is a bit much. "Is it okay if we video call? It helps to see faces when people talk."

"That's fine. One sec."

I pull the phone away from my ear and see the video request pop up. I turn on my lamp and prop the phone up against the base before I answer it.

"Better?" he asks. When his face pops up, he's laying down

in his bed with his phone directly above him. He's wearing his infamous glasses, and they're round. Scandalous!

"Much better." I smile and lay down on the pillow so my face is in frame. "Your glasses?"

He sucks in a breath of air, probably expecting the worst from me, and I'm prepared to deliver. "Are they bad?"

"No, they look good on you. You know what they say about boys who wear round glasses?" I grin. Although our friendship is new, I feel like I can start teasing him.

"Judging by that look, it's something bad."

"It is." I wiggle my eyebrows.

"I don't want to know then." He smiles.

"Fine." I put my palms up in surrender. "I'll spare you."

His smile softens a little when he asks, "You seem like you're in a better mood?"

"I am." I nod. "Mom stayed home with me today, and she's been feeding me and stuff."

"Good. Is everything better between you two?" he asks.

"I think so. Yeah."

He smiles but then he stares into the camera, waiting. I realize he probably doesn't want to pry too much or dig too deep too fast.

"Um...it was a driving lesson. With Sam," I swallow. "I almost hit a deer and all I could think about—"

"Was your dad," he finished, realizing what could've triggered the panic attack.

"Yeah, that's how he died, and I could've died, and it just seems so…easy," I exhale. "It's so easy to die. It's a miracle any of us are alive, really? I hope that makes sense. I'm not sure how to phrase it."

"I understand," he affirms so quietly I almost don't hear him.

"I guess I was so caught up on not being left behind that I forgot why I avoided getting my license in the first place." I got my permit when I turned fifteen. It was a multiple choice test so that was easy.

"It's not a big deal if you don't get your license right away."

"Says the licensed driver."

"Okay, but I didn't have—I—" he exhales forcefully, trying to collect his thoughts. "So pottery? It's not the first thing I've tried. I've tried video games, baking, painting, guitar, hiking. And I failed at all of them. I was really bad, but I knew that I'd be good at something so I kept trying and found pottery. And I'm not saying driving is like pottery, but I'm saying sometimes it takes a while to get good at something. And it's okay to be really bad at it for a while."

I close my eyes to process what he's saying. It's okay that I'm struggling to drive. It doesn't mean that I'll never learn. Like Sam told me earlier, I'll just have to go really slow, slower than I anticipated. I still don't like that I can't be great at everything immediately, but I can try and be bad at something temporarily. I think that's doable.

"Thank you," I finally say. "How are you so good at this?"

"I'm not," he admits. "My sister has anxiety, and she has panic attacks sometimes so we've had to learn how to talk her through it. It's taught me to not try so hard and take things so seriously, otherwise, I'd be having panic attacks too."

He chuckles softly, and I smile. "Well, you seem like a pretty good brother. A better brother than mine," I joke. Markese is perfect.

"She's the only sister I got."

"Do you miss her?"

"Sometimes." The corner of his mouth lifts into a sad smile. "She started college a couple of years ago so I've kinda gotten used to being away from her. Not this far away, but still."

I push my lips together and lightly tap my teeth, thinking. I'm not ready to get off the phone with him.

"What about the rest of your family? Do you miss them?" From his Instagram, it looks like he has both his parents.

"I have to call my mom once a week." He laughs, and I nod. That's reasonable. I'm pretty sure if I was in another state, Mom would make me call her prob every afternoon. "And we have a family group chat so I talk to everyone regularly. But I have family here. I get to see my grandparents, and I have Amaya."

"How are your grandparents? Ms. Sue...and Mr. Reggie, right?" I pull from the memory of Mom asking about them the first time he came over.

He smiles, but he seems a bit thrown that I remembered their names. "They're good," he says. "Amaya and I go over every Sunday for dinner. Best food of my life."

"I bet." I giggle. It seems that he's really found a home here, and it makes me glad. "So what do you think of Mississippi now?"

"It's one of the strangest places I've ever lived." He laughs. "And I can't imagine being anywhere else."

I smile at his response. It's the only way to describe the warmth and joy of this state despite the undercurrents of hatred and tyranny. We live and love and celebrate despite, not because.

"Did I answer that correctly, or are you gonna get mad at me?" he teases.

"I didn't get mad at you last time. It's just you can't go into someone's home and be like 'This is the worst place in the world.'"

"I don't think I said those words, but I got you. I'm sorry."

"And I'm sorry," I apologize because there's so much to apologize for. "You were right. Mississippi has a bad reputation because it earned it, but that's not all of what Mississippi is. I hope you see that now."

He smiles. "I do."

We sit like that, staring at each other before I clear my throat. "Can I ask you something?"

"Anything."

"Why have you been so nice to me?" It's something that's always bothered me. Always sat in the back of my head. I was horrible to him earlier in the school year. If anybody treated me the way that I treated him, I would've cried and probably never left my house, but he just brushed it off and moved on.

"Do you think you don't deserve it?" he asks back instead of answering my question.

"I wasn't the nicest at the beginning of the school year so I understand if you never wanted to speak to me again."

"You didn't answer my question."

"You didn't answer mine."

He shifts on the bed, now laying on his side with the phone in front of him. "To answer your question, I think we put too much pressure on first impressions. You can do everything right, and it still ends up wrong. I've learned to give people grace. I know I need it."

"How do you know if someone deserves a second chance?"

"Most people do." He smiles. "Especially you."

I chew on my inner cheek. Usually, if I can't do everything perfectly the first time, I'm discounted or punished or yelled at. It's nice to know that someone not only thinks I needed it but actually gave me a few times to get it right.

"Thank you, Kamron. You're probably the kindest person I've ever met."

"You deserve it."

I have to squeeze my lips together to stop the cheeky grin

that wants to emerge.

"I'm glad you talked to me, but I don't want to hold you too much longer—" The grin releases because he's already starting to sound like a Southerner—"Can I call you tomorrow? Video call?"

"Yeah, you can."

He smiles again. "Perfect. Talk to you later."

I wave at the camera before tapping the red button and watching his face vanish. Between the grinning and blushing, my cheeks tingle so bad that I have to press my palms against them to calm them down. These feelings I have for Kamron Barksdale are going to ruin me.

Chapter Twenty

The afternoon of the homecoming dance, I slather the cool water on my face, dry it and then apply sunscreen. I dab a dot of concealer under my eyes, around my mouth, and between my brows and use my fingers to blend it in. Then I apply bronzer around the corners of my face and on my eyelids before adding blush to my cheeks, nose, and brow bones. I'm not coordinated enough to do eye makeup so I leave that for Luna. The cocoa tinted lip gloss completes the look.

My hair is already parted down the middle from when I washed my hair yesterday, so I add a star clip to each side that I picked up from the hair store. I grab my vanilla musk perfume and spray a tiny amount on my wrists and knees. That is the most I can handle without getting a migraine. Going to my closet, I grab the silver gown and let the silky texture glide over my fingers. I step into the dress and shimmy it up over my body. Looking in my floor-length mirror, it's like I, myself, am the star.

I grab my silver sandals to wear with my dress and walk

downstairs.

"Naima," Mom gasps. "You're gorgeous."

"Thanks, Mom," I beam.

Markese looks up from the YouTube video he's watching on the couch and then back to his video. "You look a'ight," he mumbles.

"Thanks, Bug!" I pinch his cheeks, and he squirms under me.

"Let me take a picture," Mom says, reaching for her phone.

I roll my eyes but oblige, putting forward my best model poses in the living room. When she finishes, she says they're perfect so I grab a couple of N95 masks before sliding my feet into my Crocs, putting my sandals in my purse, and walking across the lawn towards Sam's house. When I get there, Ms. Tish can't keep her hands off of me and excessively compliments my hair and my dress. I walk back to Sam's room, and he's in his boxers with his shirt half buttoned, fumbling with his tie. His curly hair is still damp.

He sees me in the doorway. "Good, you're here. Can you help me please?"

"With what part?"

He looks down at his body and then back up at me. "I should get dressed, right?"

"Yeah." I nod and sit on his bed.

He sprays cologne on his neck, wrists, and chest. The smell of citrus and coffee float in the air with hints of a smoky woodsy note. Once the scent fills the room, everything smells like dark chocolate—smoky and sweet. Sam buttons his shirt, grabs his pants, and pulls them up, tucking his shirt in it. Looking at himself in the mirror, he slides the belt through the loops and buckles it. He looks at his hair and combs his fingers through it.

"Do you still have that foam I gave you?" I ask.

"You know I don't like adding products to my hair," he tells me while still eyeing himself in the mirror.

I sigh, hop off the bed, and go to his bathroom. Sure enough, under his sink is the half-empty bottle of hair foam that I loaned him. I bring it back to his room, pump it once in my hand, and go to put it in his hair.

"Nai, no," he protests.

"It's just a pump," I tell him. "It's not a lot, and it'll help your hair be less frizzy."

"I like it frizzy," he mumbles but acquiesces and sits down so I can work it through his hair. I rub the foam between my palms and smooth it out over his curls. It takes less than a minute to go section by section and work the product in.

"See? That wasn't so hard."

"I guess not." He looks up and down at my body. "You look nice...in your dress."

"Thanks." I chew on my inner lip. I guess we're still doing the complimenting thing. I remember his tie. "Do you still need help with—"

"Yeah." He nods, stands up, and walks towards me. "Can you tie it?"

I vaguely remember some reference I picked up from the Internet. I grab his tie and say, "Around, around, up and down." I hold one side of the tie and wrap the other side around twice before trying to loop it, but it doesn't work. I try the other way, and although it almost ties, it still isn't good enough.

"YouTube?" Sam reaches for his phone and searches for a How To video. We follow the step by step instructions. My reference isn't that far off. When I do the loop, this time it makes the perfect knot at the top.

"See? I did it." I smile up at him, still holding the tie in my hand.

"Yeah, you did." He smiles back at me. The sweetness of his cologne mixes with the heat of his neck, and the smell is luscious.

"You smell nice," I tell him. See? I can say nice things, too. I widen the gap between us to sit on his bed and trade my Crocs for sandals. "Are you ready? We have to get Luna."

He grabs his keys. As we head for the front door, Ms. Tish asks for photos of us. Sam gives her his phone as well. We stand in the front lawn in front of the dense trees that I took my Spirit Week pics in front of earlier this week. We wrap our arms around each other's waists and smile.

"Okay, and now a silly picture," Ms. Tish requests.

Sam contorts his face, and I laugh trying to do the same.

"And give her a big hug, Sam."

Sam picks me up and squeezes me, and I giggle. When he puts me down, we're looking at each other smiling.

"That's the one," Ms. Tish says and hands Sam's phone back to us. "Y'all look so cute together."

Sam thumbs through the pics before finally showing me, "I like this one."

In it, he's holding me, and we're gazing into each other's eyes, smiling.

"Yeah," I agree. "We look nice."

Ms. Tish squeezes my shoulder. "You really do look beautiful tonight, Naima. You two have fun!" She waves at us before going back in the house.

We hop in Sam's Jeep, and I put on my seat belt before I share my observation, "Why when you dress up and put on a little makeup, people come out of the wood works to tell you how much better you look? It's like they're saying that every other day I'm a raggedy bitch, but *today* I am a goddess. I'm a goddess everyday."

Sam chuckles while pushing the button to start the Jeep. "I don't think people mean it like that. It's just that you don't dress up a lot, but when you do, you look nice. You look nice every day, but especially today." He glances sideways at me.

I cross my arms because it feels like he's taking this complimenting thing too far. "Thanks," I whisper looking out the window.

I let Sam's country music fill the silence of the Jeep while we drive into town. Once we get to the city limits, I call Luna and ask if she's ready for us to pick her up.

"I'm going with Kike." There's silence. "Sorry, y'all. I guess you can be each other's dates." We stare at each other, and Sam's cheeks flush pink. That is not part of the plan. We're supposed to go as a group.

"I'll see you there!" She rushes off the phone before either of us can respond.

I shake my head in disbelief. I can't believe Luna's abandoning me.

When we get there, Luna wears her matching dress. The deep blue of the dress perfectly compliments her honey brown skin. Just as I suspected. Her hair's curled in waves, and she pins the front away from her face.

"You look beautiful," I say.

"And you look beautiful." She grabs my hand and twirls me around. Then I twirl her. Sam's taking pictures of us the whole time which he shows us. Luna grabs the phone and flips through the photos of us. "What is this?" she asks, showing us the picture from earlier that Sam liked before looking at the phone again. "It's cute."

"I think I'll post it on Instagram," Sam shares.

Our mouths gape open.

"After all these years, I finally made it," I mock-celebrate with Luna.

"I have an image to maintain," Sam says, adjusting his suit jacket.

"Ah yes, you want the girls to thirst over you, and be like, 'Sammy, do you like Black girls?'" I clutch my chest in mockery.

"Do you like Latinas?" Luna adds.

"Oh, pick me, Sammy. Pick me." I bat my eyelashes, and me and Luna laugh.

"Ha ha ha," Sam deadpans. "I don't let anyone call me Sammy except for you."

"You better not," I wag my finger at him playfully.

Somewhere in our laughter, Kike walks out of the car and joins us. He stands at nearly six feet tall with raven black curly hair, a broad nose, and bushy brows. When he smiles, I see exactly what Luna sees in him.

"Hey, I'm Kike," he says, reaching his hand out for mine.

I reach out to awkwardly shake his hand. "Naima. It's nice to finally meet you. I've heard so much about you," I say. I turn my head to mouth to Luna: *He's pretty.*

"Yeah, same here," Kike says.

Kike and Sam start talking, and I wrap my arm around Luna's. "Okay, I forgive you now for abandoning me."

"Girl," she says, playfully pushing my arm and rolling her eyes.

We put on our masks before we go into the building. Luna offers to do my eyebrows and false lashes in the bathroom.

Since it's the only part people will see, I want it to look good. As she fills in the second brow, she asks, "Do you think Kamron's coming?"

"I don't know," I sigh. I hope he's coming, but I was afraid that I'd be coming off too strong if I asked yesterday when he called again. "We've been video calling."

She hits me with the makeup bag.

"Why didn't you tell me?!"

I shush her because there are other girls in the stalls.

"I mean we're friends, and it's not like I tell you or Sam when the other video calls me."

"¡Dios mío, Naima! Kamron is not just a friend. He *likes* you."

"Mom said the same thing," I grimace.

Pinching the lash between her fingers, her head tilts like *I told you so*. I gnaw my bottom lips because I kinda want it to mean something, but why hasn't he said anything? I've been too afraid to bring up the kiss, and he hasn't either. We just skated over that. I wish he'd be honest and direct with me. I'm just scared that I'm wrong, and if I'm wrong, he's never gonna speak to me again, and that's the last thing I want.

"Do you like him?" Luna whispers. She puts glue on the lash and waves it to make it tacky.

When I think about him, a warmth ripples across my chest and belly. His smile is kind, and he's been so patient with me—more patient than I think I'm afforded.

"There's something about him, that's so—" I exhale, struggling to find the right words and realize "About the Boy" is perfect so I sing it. Luna rolls her eyes, but I have to finish the repeating chorus. I clap to commend my performance. There's a Little Mix song for every occasion.

Luna grabs my arms to steady me. "Okay, enough singing. You like him. I got it."

"I do," I admit and smile. Now what am I gonna do with that admission?

Luna finishes applying the lashes before we leave the bathroom to go find our dates. The room is lit with black light. String lights and cotton hang from the ceiling to simulate clouds and stars. Gold and silver balloons cover the floor near the walls, and plastic stars adhere to the wall. I twirl between the chairs thinking about how unbelievably beautiful it is. Sam finds us and greets me by placing his hand on my lower back.

"Y'all okay? You were in the bathroom a *long* time."

"You're in girls' business," I say.

"Yeah!" Luna hypes me up.

Sam rears back at my sassiness then shrugs because we're weirdos. "Well, Kike went over there." He points past Luna. "I'm gonna be with the boys if you need me." He looks to me for approval. He's taking this date thing seriously.

"Yeah, that's fine." I wave him away and watch as he walks towards his friends, and Luna walks over to Kike.

I sit down at a table and pull out my phone. Sam tagged me

in an Instagram photo with a caption of three star emojis. I click on it. In the darkness of the room, we look happy and comfortable in a way that warms my heart. I smile at the photo and then scroll down to the comments. Sure enough, there are dozens of comments talking about the fact that not only did Sam post a girl, but a Black girl. People are so predictable.

I shake my head and search for Kamron's username. His story is active with the regular pink ring around his profile pic. I click on it and see that he's finished a teapot. It's similar to the picture he showed me a few weeks ago except this one is a forest green instead of a mint blue. He captions it "just finished," and the story was posted three hours ago. I press the heart at the bottom of the story.

The DJ announces himself and gives a spiel that I tune out to study Kamron's Instagram. Hands pull at my shoulder to try and get me up. I turn around and see Luna who wants me to dance with her. I begrudgingly get up, but after a few minutes, he plays a song from Beyoncé's *Renaissance.* I grab Luna's hand as we both shake our hips to the beat. We have to be careful not to twerk; the chaperones break up any dancing they view as unholy.

"Move" starts playing, and my feet bounce on the floor because the DJ not only knows a Little Mix song, but an older one at that. Sam taps me on the shoulder.

"You did this?" I ask.

He nods and smiles. "Can't waste a good song."

I hug his neck to thank him. When I pull away, his hand is there for me to grab. He twirls me around, and I stand on my tippy toes to try and twirl him. He awkwardly ducks under his own arm to complete the turn. He shakes his butt, and we all laugh at him. Then, he moves towards me, clasping one of my hands and grabbing my waist with the other. When he pulls me close to him, my stomach drops so I laugh and gently push his chest to hide my nervousness. Sam's grip softens on my lower back, and when I gaze up at him, his stare unsettles me, like the energy is off. *Does he?* I squint trying to decipher it. No. I push the thought away.

When the song ends, Sam declares he's sitting down like he's tired even though he tries a new dance every week. We watch Sam return to his friends leaning against the wall.

"What was that?" Luna asks me.

"I don't know," I admit. That was weird.

With each song, our bodies convulse more and more. Sweat builds up in our masks, on our foreheads, necks, and back, but we don't care; we're having fun. Once the DJ switches to a slow song, Luna goes to find Kike, and I search for Sam. We see each other at the same time, and as I'm making my way to him, someone grabs my arm. I turn around to find Kamron.

His hand is outstretched. "Will you dance with me?"

I blink, trying to process what's going on. He's wearing a fitted dark blue suit with a white dress shirt. No tie. Most of his face is obscured by his mask, but his hand is out, waiting for mine.

I take it. It's been over two weeks since I've seen him in person. He's gotten a fresh fade, and although I can't see most of his face, I know it's beautiful. His stare is deep, and my chest flutters in response, but I stay. He clasps my fingers and brings them up in the air. He curves his other arm out, holding it. Waiting.

"Is it okay if I—" He looks down at his arm that he wants to wrap around my waist.

"Yeah. That's fine," I reassure him. His hand holds my lower back. Although his touch is gentle, it's enough to shimmer around my waist and trickle down my thighs. I turn back to him as his soft brown eyes take in my face, my hair, and then my dress.

"Naima," he says. "You're stunning."

Stunning? The word stings my lips and flutters out to my cheeks. I gnaw on my bottom lip in an attempt to tamper down the sensation. My brain flips through all the responses I could say, but I really only have one question.

"What are you doing here?"

His gaze flickers towards mine, thinking, before he averts it and says, "I wanted to see you."

His words, a whoosh. I can't misinterpret this, can I? Why would he want to see me? He has to like me. My eyes jump from his mask, his eyes, to the people around us. They're either at the tables on their phones or lovingly staring into the eyes of their dates. I want to respond to Kamron, but I don't even know where to begin.

"Why?" I ask. Is it good? Is it bad? Why would he want to see me? Why now? Why couldn't he wait until we're back at school?

Now it's him looking around the room. Watching the side of his face, his eye lashes are more prominent, still pretty. His jaw peeks out from his mask, and I have the growing desire to caress the side of his face. Rub my thumb at the freshly cut part of his scalp above his ear. Feel the prickliness of it. My arm is around his neck so I feel when he breathes in. He's thinking, but I don't.

"I like you," I blurt out, my breath no longer tight as the honesty releases the pressure from my chest.

When he turns back to look at me, the fear comes. I said the unspeakable thing. While I feel better, now he may never speak to me again. He may call me a weirdo, and he won't sit beside me in science class anymore. He won't play with my fingers while he holds my hand. He may ask Mrs. Truss for a new partner, and I'll have to spend the rest of the school year avoiding him and his gaze, knowing that he thinks I'm some awkward weirdo that he doesn't want to be around.

"Can we talk outside?"

Anxiety flip flops in my stomach. I messed up. This is the part where he says he never wants to talk to me again. He takes his hands off of me, steps back, and gestures for me to walk in front of him. I do—squeezing my thumb in front of me as I walk into the hallway. There's a bench that I walk to and sit. He joins me, turning his body so he faces me. He takes his mask off. "I'm negative. I hope it's okay?" he asks.

I nod but keep mine on. My shoulders stiffen as I gaze down at my fidgeting fingers, awaiting his disgust.

"It was really loud in there, and I um—"

I squeeze my eyes shut, trying to bear the intensity of my heart thumping in my ears and prepare for his incoming rejection.

"Naima." His finger is under my chin, and he gently lifts it. I open my eyes to see him staring at me. A slight smile on his face. "I like you, too."

Under his steady gaze, my heart flutters hearing his words. I didn't misinterpret anything. I was right. He likes me, and I like him. I stare at him bearing the heat that spreads across my cheeks and chest, not sure what to do next.

He drops his finger and scratches the side of his head, glancing at the wall before he speaks. "I wanted to ask you out a few weeks ago after we finished our project, but I don't know how long—" He looks up at the ceiling and sighs. "How long I'll be in Mississippi, and I didn't want to hurt you down the line by leaving."

"What are you saying?"

"I'm saying I can't make promises about how long I'll be here, but" —he grabs my hand— "I wanna take you out. On a date."

I gasp.

"Only if you want to. No pressure."

"I'd love to." I smile.

"Really?" His shoulders loosen before he clutches his chest in relief. "That was the scariest thing I ever had to do."

"Did you think I'd say no?" I ask, lifting an eyebrow. I kinda risked everything to tell him I liked him first.

"I never know what to think about you." He grins but then taps his finger to his bottom lip. "I also didn't think I'd get this far. Now I gotta think of a date."

"You don't have anything planned?" My mouth gapes in faux shock though he can't see it.

"It's gonna be great. I promise." He flashes a smile before covering it up with his mask. He stands up then holds his hand out for me. "Wanna go back in there?"

"I'd love to," I say, grabbing his hand and following him back to the dance floor.

Luna joins us and wiggles her eyebrows. I nod, letting her know that she was right about him. She reaches her arm around my neck and hugs me. In my ear, she whispers, "I'm so happy for you."

Kike walks over, and the four of us dance in a circle to the music until the DJ announces that it's the last song. It's the Cupid Shuffle—a line dance that old people love to play at family reunions and weddings. I hate any song that tells me to go right or left, but when Kamron bumps my shoulder to join him, I do.

We stand next to each other on the border of the crowd. I follow his lead, kicking whichever foot he does and moving to wherever side he goes. This is a foolproof method until the group shifts where I'm at the front of the line, and I panic. Luckily, I see Sam and instead of dancing, I wave him over to avoid looking like a fool.

As he gets closer to me, he kicks his legs out to the song and eventually shuffles his way into the crowd. I laugh at his silliness. We shuffle some more until the music stops. Everyone on the dance floor claps while the DJ essentially tells us that we don't have to go home, but we can't stay here. Luna, Kike, Kamron, and I walk outside of the building, and everyone takes off their masks. I inhale the soft chill of the night air and rub the goosebumps that rise on my arms. Kamron appears beside me.

"I had fun." His hands are tucked in the pockets of his pants.

"See? I told you Homecoming is fun." I grin.

We walk gingerly under the school's flood lights, wanting to delay the inevitable ending. I watch the ground. My sandals peek from under my dress with each step when I hear a camera shutter.

"Shit." I look over at Luna whose phone is in front of her face. I give her a *Really?* look. "You looked soooo cute, Naima," she tries to explain so hopefully Kamron doesn't think she's a creep.

Instead he chuckles and asks, "Do you want to take a pic of us?"

He slides his arm around my waist. Next to him, I can smell the faint scent of the warehouse he got his suit from. I debate the appropriate closeness to a boy that I kissed and said I liked and who said he liked me back and decide that maybe if I move too close too fast it'll repulse him so I leave a small gap between our hips.

Luna walks over and shows us the pics she took. I look nervous and not great, but Kamron says, "Beautiful. Can you send those to me?"

As Luna occupies herself with sending the pics, Kamron leans towards my ear and whispers, "I'll see you Monday." He kisses my cheek before he turns to tell the rest of the group, "Be safe, y'all!"

I stand there, touching the part of my face that his lips graced. He kissed me. I just want to be in this moment forever. When I can no longer see him, I turn towards Luna who's beaming.

"We're gonna leave, too," Kike says, waving to me from over Luna's head. He wraps his arms around her shoulders, and they walk to his car. Then Sam walks out, laughing with Darius, Marcus, and Jeff. We say goodnight to them before he walks towards me.

"You have fun?" I ask him.

"Yeah. You?"

We walk side by side back to his Jeep. I think about Kamron saying he liked me, asking me on a date, and kissing me good-night. How despite my worst fears about him, he may actually be a dream come true. I stare up at the stars overhead that look a bit denser and brighter than usual. Magical, even. A cherry on top of a beautiful night.

"I had a blast."

CHAPTER TWENTY-ONE

Monday, Kamron sits with Luna and me at lunch. He scoots his chair a little closer than usual, and while he's talking, his thigh rubs against mine. His words shimmer in the air—many out of my grasp—because all I can focus on is the pressure of his knee against mine. I prepare myself for the next time it's going to happen and shift in my seat when it does. When the bell rings, my body follows its usual rhythms: get rid of the tray, grab books, and head to class.

Kamron walks beside me to class. I'm not sure if he says anything. Even if he did, I'd doubt I'd be able to concentrate long enough to process what he's saying. When we get to AP Bio, he sits beside me, scooting the stool closer to me again. I'm afraid to bounce my knee, afraid that it'd scare him, but since it's the first day back, I left my dodecahedron at home. I stuff my hands in my hoodie pocket and scrunch them trying to loosen the tightness building up in my arms. I inhale slowly and exhale, but it only slightly alleviates the pressure in my chest.

I stare down at my notebook trying to focus on how to release the buildup of pressure in my body without causing a scene. Kamron slides a paper towards me. I glance at where he wrote: *You ok?*

I nod, but then debate whether or not I should tell him the truth. That it's his fault I feel this way, and the swirls of emotions in my body need some kind of outlet, but I'm struggling to find it. I glance up at Mrs. Truss whose back is turned to us while she's writing on the board. I lift my pencil and write on the paper: *Need to stim.*

He nods, takes the paper back, and writes: *Walk to the bathroom?*

Great idea. I wave my hand in the air to get Mrs. Truss's attention.

"Yes, Naima?" Her voice holds the slightest edge of annoyance, but I ignore it.

Instead, I clear my throat and say, "I need to go to the bathroom."

She gestures to the bathroom pass hanging beside the door. I get up from my seat, grab it, slide it on my wrist, and rush out the door. My feet pound against the floor. Each step jostles the tension in my body, and I'm finally able to breathe. I cut through the middle hallway and walk to the cafeteria and then around the building, passing the main hall bathroom, until I feel like I can breathe somewhat normally again. I speed past AP Bio, hoping no one sees me walk past the door, and end up at the art center bathroom. I go into a stall, wipe the seat before I sit down with my clothes on. Pulling my phone out of my pocket, I text Kamron.

NAIMA: That helped. Thank you.

I open a few apps on my phone, more as a stim than to see anything specifically. His text pops up at the top of the screen.

KAMRON: No prob. You coming back? It's been ten minutes.

Shit.

That's probably what everyone else thinks I'm doing anyway, especially the way I rushed out of the room. I exhale rising up from the toilet and walk to the sink to wash my hands. Walking back to the class slowly, I breathe deeply to hopefully survive the rest of class. When I open the door, I slide the pass off my wrist and hang it back on the wall and slip beside Kamron.

He leans over and whispers, "You good?"

I nod. Then he slides the paper back towards me. On it, he wrote: *Can I take you home after school?*

Behind the words are indentations left from all the different ways he tried to ask the same question, but erased it. I smile, thinking about how nervous he must be around me, too.

I write under the question: *yes.*

After the last bell, I walk towards the parking lot to meet

Kamron, but Sam's there waiting for me. He turns expecting for me to join him, but I don't. Instead Kamron shows up next to me.

"Nai?" Sam asks.

"I'm taking her home," Kamron explains. "Just for today, and she's all yours tomorrow."

Sam's eyebrows draw together, wondering what's going on. He stares at me then Kamron.

"I'll be fine, Sammy. See you at the house." I start to walk with Kamron to his car but turn around. "If I'm murdered, you know who did it!" I yell at Sam, and he rolls his eyes at me.

"You think I'd murder you?" Kamron asks, slightly offended.

"I never know what anyone's gonna do," I admit. "But I hope for the best."

We slide into his car, and I put on the seat belt. When he turns on the car, the middle of a podcast turns on. I can't make out what it's about before he grabs his phone and switches to one of his personal playlist. Masego plays.

"Sorry about that."

"No worries." I squeeze my hands tightly between my thighs to calm the growing worries in my body. It's the first time I'm alone...with Kamron...in an enclosed space since we said we liked each other.

Once he navigates his way through the parking lot and off of school grounds, he finally asks me, "Have you ever seen

Heartbreak High?"

"No," I giggle. Did he really want to take me home to talk about a TV show?

"Well there's this girl Quinni and she's a um...person...with autism."

"Autistic person," I correct him. Autism is not a disease people carry. It's a neurotype—a different way of experiencing the world.

"Sorry. Is that bad?" He wrinkles his nose.

"No. It's fine. It's just that you don't say, 'person with Blackness.' You say 'Black person.' It's the same."

"Sorry. Okay, Quinni's an *autistic person*, and she goes out on a date with this girl and *hates* it," he explains.

"Where was the date?"

"In a restaurant."

I nod, understanding exactly what she went through. "So it was the noise and lights and smells, and she had trouble concentrating?" I ask.

"Right! And I was just wondering if there were sensory things that I should look out for? For our date?"

"Oh." That's really thoughtful of him. "Um...I tend to be sensory avoiding for most things. I hate loud noises, bright lights, strong smells. Especially perfumes and flowers and stuff."

"Like cologne?"

The memory of me calling him annoying strikes my chest,

and I squeeze my eyes shut, ashamed. "Yeah. I'm sorry about that. You're not annoying, and you didn't know how it would affect me. It's not your fault."

"I didn't make you sick or anything, did I?" He glances away from the road to look at me.

"I did have a migraine" —I purse my lips before deciding to add—"Because of you."

He sucks in air and then taps the steering wheel. "I can see how that's annoying."

"I'm okay with cologne though." I rush to add, trying not to make him feel bad. "It's just less is more."

He nods and then counts on his fingers. "Okay so no loud noises, bright lights, and strong smells."

There are two senses left.

"Taste. I don't eat eggs or seafood. It feels really gross and rubbery in my mouth. I do like crunchy foods."

"Okay hearing, sight, smell, taste." He has four fingers in the air. "What about touch?"

"I am actually a touch seeker. That's why my friends are always holding me or rubbing me. Touch is like sunshine and sparkles. I just need something touching my skin always."

"Touch seeker. Got it." He nods his head. His eyebrows scrunches together. "How do you avoid all of this stuff? At school?"

"Oh." His question throws me off so I tug at the hem of my shirt. No one bothers to ask me how I survive every day. I'm just expected to.

"I tend to take classes with big windows. It helps a lot to diffuse the lights. Also the yellow lights they use are much better than the white or blue ones so I try to take classes where I know they have yellow lights. If I can't, I just try and power through it." I thought through the most aggravating senses I work to numb. "Usually people don't wear loud perfumes to school. I try to sit in a corner of the classroom instead of the middle to avoid feeling claustrophobic. Finding ways to stim when I need to is really the hardest part. I try to bring a fidget toy, but sometimes I forget."

Autism is such a complex experience; it's really hard to distill it down to dos and don'ts. My needs vary from day to day so while I may be able to tolerate something one day, I absolutely can't the next. When I look ahead through the windshield, I see we are nearing the intersection that takes us out of city limits. Just minutes away from my house.

"It seems...exhausting," he says.

"It is," I exhale. "I sleep ten hours a night."

"*Ten* hours?"

"Yeah, and a nap thrown in if I can help it." Outside the window, we pass the farms and forests. Leaves are starting to yellow. It's only a couple more weeks until the trees are in full fall form. "Is this gonna be hard for you?" I ask with a smile tugging my lips. Is he up for the challenge is what I really want to know.

"Not at all. I think my original plan still works."

He turns into our driveway, and I grab my book bag from beside my legs. "I'm excited to see what you pull off."

"I think you'll like it." He looks me up and down before grinning. His canines sit atop his bottom lip, and my heart flip flops in response.

"I'll see you tomorrow at school."

I smile and start to shut the door when he yells, "Have a good night!"

"You too!" I yell back while walking towards the house, embracing the warmth that's building in my tummy. In the corner of my eye, I see Sam's shoes peeking out the corner of the porch.

"I'm alive," I announce to Sam with my arms wide. He gives a half smile while he's leaning back in the swing, his hands stuffed in his pockets. I slide next to him.

"I see," he says. He glances down at me, his eyes assessing. His mouth opens with a question but closes out of fear. What's up with these two? They act like they're divorced parents, and I'm the child they're shuffling back and forth.

"What's wrong?" I ask.

His brow furrows, and he tilts his head. He points back towards the driveway. "What's going on there?"

My stomach drops. It's a conversation I always avoided with him mainly because it's awkward to talk to one guy about another guy. Luna has dated boys; Sam hasn't, so it makes more sense to go to her about these things.

"He...asked...me out on a date." My fingers twist on each other like vines.

"Oh," he says. "And what did you say?"

I shake my head and smile. "Yes." What else would I say?

"Are you sure that's a good idea?"

My face scrunches while I reel back from his question. What does he mean is that a good idea? It's a good idea because it's what I want. He's not even looking at me. His head is tilted toward the ceiling of the porch.

"Sam—"

"I'm just saying. Nai, we don't know this guy. He could be dangerous."

His hands grab mine with his plea, but I snatch my arm back.

"Where is this coming from?"

He swivels, his back against the swing again. "I just don't get why'd you go out on a date with someone you barely even know."

I scowl. "And how well do you know the girls you go out on a date with?"

His head leans against the swing, and he sighs. His voice softens. "That's different."

"How?"

Don't say because I'm a girl and you're a boy.

"It just is. Boys are dangerous, and they lie. I'm looking out for you."

He rests his elbows on his thighs, and I stare at the back of his head. It was his fault that I second guessed myself with Kamron in the first place. His insistence that I misinterpret everything, but I interpret just fine. He's always hovering, making me question myself and when I have one nice thing—a date—he wants to take that away from me, too. He wants me to keep second guessing myself.

I hop out of the swing, heading to the back door when he grabs my wrist.

"Nai, I don't want to fight with you."

I'm facing away from him when I say, "I can't tell." I know he hears the tears in my voice. He knows exactly what he's doing.

While still grasping my wrist, he gets up from the swing, grabs my shoulder and turns me around so we're standing face to face.

"Nai." His hands on either side of my face. I gaze out past the yard towards the woods bordering it. Anything is better than looking at him. "I care about you, and I don't want to see you hurt."

Hot tears burn the corners of my eyes, but I don't lift my gaze from the evergreen trees on the outer edge of the yard.

"Nai." His voice is soft but demanding. "Say something."

My jaw clenches. "You're treating me like a child," I say, and then turn my gaze towards him. I feel my face hardening. I know he knows how angry I am at him. How dare he try and tell me what I can and can't do?

He removes his palms from my cheeks and steps back. He lifts his arms and acquiesces. "Okay," he whispers and stares towards the wall. His eyes flicking back and forth, wondering.

I exhale to loosen the stiffness in my face and sit down on the swing, covering my face with my hands. He sits beside me and rubs my back. I hate how much it helps.

"I'm not a child, Sam." My hands muffle the words. "I can make my own decisions."

"You can," he agrees.

"Well right now it seems like you think you know better than me."

Silence. He does think he knows better than me. I turn towards him in disbelief. Does he really view me as incompetent?

The birds chirping and the occasional car on the highway fills in the silence between us. He closes his eyes, exhales, and then turns towards me. Holding my hands in his, he says, "I'm sorry."

With downward eyes, I bite my lip. Sorry is nice, but it does little to tamper the growing resentment in my body. The disgust that my own friend doesn't trust me to live my life for myself. This is why I talk to Luna. At least she supports my decisions instead of questioning them.

"You're still angry."

What an astute fucking observation.

I rise from the bench and pace in front of it. "Of course I'm still angry. You don't trust me."

"It's not that I don't trust you. I don't trust him."

"Well I do." I stop in front of him, and he lifts his eyes to meet mine. "I trust Kamron so trust me."

He doesn't say anything. His hands are clasped in front of him. My chest still heaves, and I will it to slow. He leans in the swing and places an arm over the back before asking, "Do you like him?"

I blink away the heat rising in my chest and throat, drying my mouth. "Yes," I say and fold my arms, leaning against the support beam.

"Okay." His voice is tight, but I know he wants to move on.

My shoulders sink because I don't want to be mad at him. I gaze up at the ceiling, trying to find the words I want to say. My foot taps the porch. "It really hurts me...that you don't believe I can make good decisions, Sam."

I see he wants to protest, but I shake my head for him to let me finish and sit down beside him.

"This is very new for me, and I want to be excited. It hurts that you'd try to take that away from me." His lips twist in response. "And I'm not saying I'm gonna marry the guy or anything. It's one date. Who knows? It could be a bad date, but I'd like to try."

I reach my hands out to his as a peace offering. He accepts. "Okay," he nods. "But let me know if he does *anything* to make you uncomfortable."

"I'm always uncomfortable," I snort.

"More uncomfortable than usual," he adds.

"I don't think there's a meter for my discomfort. It's just a constant stream of being uncomfortable."

He laughs, and I'm thankful that we've sliced through the tension, that I spoke my peace, and that he listened.

Squeezing his hands, I say, "Thank you for being here and thank you for caring about me."

His eyes glisten so I grab the nape of his neck and kiss his temple. He smiles softly then says, "I kinda feel like you shouldn't be doing that if you're going on dates with other boys."

"That's silly."

He shrugs. "Guys get jealous. I'm just warning you."

"But I've literally gotten hugs and kissies from you for years. I'm supposed to just stop? Because of a date?" That doesn't make sense to me. If I can't hug and kiss the people I love, how will they know I love them?

"Some people can be a little" —he inhales thinking of his next word— "territorial."

"I'm not property."

"I know," he sighs.

"It's ego." I recall our conversation from a couple of months ago about love. I lean back against the swing. "People think they can fulfill your every need, but it's not realistic. Imagine me demanding all my love and affection from one person. That'd be asking for too much."

He chuckles. "Trust me. I know."

My face softens, but my eyes squint. Is he calling me needy?

A gentle breeze blows against us causing our curls to float above our heads. He exhales and gently pushes his shoulder into mine. "So, are you ready for your date?"

I smile and gaze up at him. "I am."

I can't wait to see what Kamron planned for us.

Chapter Twenty-Two

Kamron shows up Saturday about an hour before our date is supposed to start. He tells me to wear something comfortable. The sun's already setting when I catch him carrying supplies from his car to a section of the yard past my garden. After he's done, he comes and gets me from the house. I'm wearing a long-sleeved crop top, joggers, socks, and my Crocs.

The cicadas hum as he takes my hand and leads me to the spot that he's set up. There's a queen size blanket on the ground with a citronella candle at each corner to keep the mosquitoes at bay. On the oversized blanket are pillows and a few throw blankets. A picnic basket sits in the middle of the blanket.

"When you were talking about the stars the other day, it reminded me of the last time I was at the planetarium with my family a few years ago. So I wanted to bring the planetarium to you." He spreads his arms out to showcase his work.

"You know there's a planetarium in Jackson? It's one of the

largest ones in the country," I inform him.

"I...will remember that for next time" —he smiles— "but this one is in your backyard." He ushers me onto the palette and places pillows to suggest that I lay down.

I slide my Crocs off and pull a blanket over my body. "What's in the basket?" I ask him.

"Lunchables and Capri suns."

I laugh, noticing how much detail he put into this date. There's no bright lights, muted smells, nature noises, crunchy foods, and plenty of blankets to wrap myself in. A crescent moon floats in the sky so it's much easier to see the stars above the wild outline of trees.

He fumbles with his phone, handing me one of his wireless ear buds. A whiff of patchouli, citrus, and lavender passes my nose, like the sweet woodsy smell of a bonfire. It's cozy but luxurious.

"Your cologne smells nice," I say.

"It's not too much?"

"No, it's perfect." I beam.

He slides down beside me, and an Australian or New Zealander lady starts speaking. He puts the other bud in his ear and nervously grins. We gaze up at the sky. The speaker teaches us how to find a planet. I always knew it was possible, but I became giddy when I actually found it: Venus. The lady says that Venus was named after the Goddess of Love, and I feel when Kamron's eyes turn to me. I gulp down the heat rising in my throat and fidget with my fingers under the blanket.

The woman tries to help us find Orion, but we aren't in the Southeastern hemisphere so we don't see it. We still listen to her story about Orion and the Orion nebula—how Orion is filled with both young and old stars. Hearing her talk about the life cycle of the star reminds me of the life cycle of Earth. How everything that exists must live, burn bright, and then die. It's oddly comforting that this little time we have on Earth is part of the universe's design. A gift, really.

When the audio stops, Kamron grabs his phone. "I'm sorry about that. I should've listened to the full episode to know we don't even have Orion."

"That's fine." I lift myself with my arms behind me. "Hearing about Orion reminded me how death and life exist simultaneously. It's timely."

He grins. "Yeah, it was like what we were talking about the other day. How death is not the end because energy can never be destroyed. So even if a star dies, it'll always come back as something else."

I nod then smile because that's exactly how I feel. While death is an ending; it's not the end. Nothing ever truly dies.

He looks back at his phone and says, "There's something else I wanted to show you." He lays down again with his phone facing the sky. "It's an app that tells you what the different constellations are."

He leans towards me so we both could see his phone. The

first constellation we see is Cassiopeia. It's shaped like a W. I look up from the phone to actually see it in the sky. Kamron moves the phone around, and it tells us that it's hovering under Perseus. He moves the phone some more until we see the V of Pisces.

I gasp, "That's my sign!"

"You're a Pisces?" he asks.

"Yeah I'm a Pisces rising. Under the Tropical or western zodiac, I'm a Pisces sun, but under the sidereal, I'm an Aquarius sun. I heard the Tropical is a more colonial view of astrology, and it's super patriarchal because it prioritizes the sun which is masculine instead of seeing the sun and the moon as two parts of a whole. But also the rising is supposed to be a more accurate way of viewing yourself as a whole being instead of making your identity this piece of a whole."

I glance at him to see if he understood, and his eyes are studying me.

"I'm sorry. Astrology was a special interest a few summers ago."

"No, that's fine." He flashes his smile, and I mimic it. "I like hearing you talk."

My God. A tingle grows on the side of my face and stiffens my tongue, losing my ability to speak at all.

"Yeah, um," I blink. "What—What's your sign?"

"I don't want to say." He scratches his temple.

"You're either a Scorpio or a Gemini," I giggle. "Don't worry, Luna's a Scorpio, and we get along well."

"I'm a Gemini." He wrinkles his nose then rolls onto his side, propping the side of his face in his hand.

I shake my head. "It's nothing to be worried about. It's just space racism," I laugh, remembering that term I picked up off of social media. "Everyone has prejudices against signs and they're not warranted. Most of us have many signs in our charts so it's silly to say one sign is better than the other."

"Yeah. I don't know my chart," he admits.

I gasp, "Do you know what time you were born?" Peeking at someone's chart is like peeking into their brain, and I'd love to know what's inside Kamron's head.

He shakes his head. "I'd have to ask my mama."

I cock my head to the side after processing what he said earlier. "Wait, you're a Gemini, and you're sixteen?"

"Mmm-hmm." His head's resting on his hand.

I lay down too so we're face to face. "That means I'm older than you. So I'm like an authority figure." I tease.

"I thought you said age doesn't equal authority."

"Oh, I think I can make an exception." I smirk.

His eyes trail down my body and back up to my face. "Is that right?"

I slide a little closer to him and smile. "Yeah, that's right."

His hand grabs mine, and he brings it to his lips. Sparkles spread across my skin, making me feel like a princess. He gently tugs to pull me so close to him that I could feel his breath on my lips. The warm smell of watermelon Ice Breaker wafts from his tongue, and the anticipation bubbles up in my chest until I can't take it anymore.

"Is it okay if I—" he asks.

"Mmm-hmmm." I interrupt him leaning in closer, centimeters from his lips.

He meets me the rest of the way. His soft lips touch mine once again. It's like they belong there. I reach for his nape, bringing him closer to me. His arms wrap around my waist to pull me into him. We separate, gasping for air, and his hand cups my jaw. Using his thumb, he caresses my cheek. I close my eyes to savor his touch. He leans in for a quick peck on my lips and exhales.

"I been waiting *forever* to do that," he whispers.

"Technically we already kissed." I slip into the nook between his arm and body.

"*Technically*, you kissed me."

I cringe. "I'm sorry. I should've asked for permission and made sure you were okay with—"

"Hey." He hooks a finger under my chin. "*I* wanted to kiss *you*. You just beat me to it."

He brings my lips to his, and a quick zap dances around my mouth. His eyes are soft when they meet mine, and he caresses my cheek again. Then his hands go back to my hand, and he starts playing with my fingers. Trails of euphoria dance on my skin.

"What does it feel like when I do this?" he asks, studying my hands.

"Divine," I tell him. "Like this is what the world was made for."

His finger slides from my wrist up my arm to my neck and eventually caresses my cheek. He pulls me closer to softly kiss me under my ears. It tickles, and tingles radiate from the spot.

"And this?" he asks.

"I didn't really feel anything." I grin. "Maybe you should try again."

"Oh really?" I can hear the smile in his heavy voice as he kisses me again on my cheek and then my nose, forehead, and finally my lips. "Feel anything that time?"

I put my index finger and thumb close together. "A little bit."

"Hmm," he says. One of his arms is under my waist, holding me against his body and with his other hand, he strokes my cheek and scans my face. Holding my jaw, he brings my lips to his and kisses me deeper. I tug at his body until he's on top of me. He kisses my jaw and then my neck before a muffled moan escapes my lips. He pulls back from me, examines me, and then smiles. "No, you felt that."

"Fine," I exhale.

He draws my face closer to his and says, "I thought so." Each word grazes my lips as he says it. He grins and draws me into him, before we lay down side by side on the blanket. I curl into his chest, and he cradles me as we lay under the stars.

CHAPTER TWENTY-THREE

"And then what happened?" Luna's face is inches from the camera after I tell her about my first date last night. Nellie meows loudly in the background.

I hug my blanket tighter over my shoulders, bite my lip, and smile. My cheeks flitter as I say, "I don't know. We just sat under the stars and talked."

I don't remember half of what he was saying because I was distracted. I can still smell his cologne in my nose, taste the mint on my tongue, and feel his phantom kisses on my skin. Making out is the best thing in the world. It feels like when Tinkerbell zooms up in the sky, and she's covered in pixie dust. All of that, the flying, the magic, the speed.

Luna squeals. "Did he ask you to be his girlfriend?"

I furrow my brow. "No." Was he supposed to?

"You have to talk to him about it. Don't be too direct. Just like, 'Hey what are we'?" She softens her face and flutters her eyelashes.

"I'm not doing all of that. It was a date, and it was good. I don't want to mess it up by being too pushy."

"I can talk to him," she offers. "I bet he's gonna sit with us at lunch tomorrow. And he's gonna have his eyes all on you."

I put my blanket over my head and draw it tight around my neck to contain the bubbling energy building up in my body. How do I deal with this feeling of a guy I like liking me back? It's too intense.

"Please don't talk to him. I'll talk to him about it, but I want to wait and make sure he *likes me* likes me. I don't want to rush it."

Frustrated, she leans her head back, "Girl, it'll be the end of the year before he's your boyfriend."

"I just want to be certain before I ask him anything."

"Okay." She rolls her eyes. She's gonna say something to him before I do. "But you can't stop me from talking to him at lunch."

～ele～

Before Kamron sits down at the table, he leans towards my ear and whispers, "Hey."

I say, "Hi," but the words are barely audible, so many butterflies are fluttering around in my throat.

He scoots his chair close to me and says in his signature strong staccato, "I had fun Saturday."

"Me too," I say, relishing the prickly feeling in my cheeks.

Nervously, I look up from my tray towards him, and he's studying my face. His hand reaches for mine under the table, and he brings it up to his lips and kisses my knuckles. He holds my fingers, and we stare, hungry for each other.

"Y'all are at school." Luna's voice is tight. Kamron laughs, and I cover my face in shame. He places his hand on my thigh, perhaps to soothe me, but it makes it worse.

"How was your date Saturday?" Luna asks Kamron.

"It was" —he pauses, trying to think of the right word— "magnificent."

"Magnificent?" I ask. That's a big word for a little ole date.

"Splendid," he says the word slowly, watching its effect on my face. "Glorious. Spectacular. Sumpt—" he stops, using one of his feet to scratch the other.

"You okay?" I ask.

"Yeah," he grunts. "Just got bit by a lot of mosquitoes."

"Have you taken allergy medicine?" Luna asks.

"And use hydrocortisone cream?" I add.

"No." He keeps scratching his foot. "Am I supposed to?"

Luna and I look at each other. Maybe I was a little too quick to say he sounded like a Southerner, because he doesn't act like one. "Come to my house after school, okay?"

He nods and agrees.

When we get to my house, I walk towards the door when

Kamron calls to me. "You dropped something."

I turn around to see him shuffling towards me. I look down at the gravel and don't really see anything besides rocks.

"It was this," he says, lifting my face with his finger and planting a kiss on me. I don't think I'll ever get used to this feeling.

"You tricked me," I whisper.

"Only a little."

"Trick me again."

He grins, and I reach for the nape of his neck, pulling his lips towards mine until that perfect zing prances along my lips. His arm reaches around my waist pulling me into him, and I wish I could melt myself into him and stay this way forever, encircled in sparkles and bliss. Unfortunately, we need to breathe, and right on cue, Kamron scratches his ankle with his other foot.

"Come on." I grab his hand, lead him into the house, and park him in the downstairs bathroom. "It'll work better if you wash your feet off first."

While he's downstairs, I run up to my bathroom to grab the hydrocortisone cream and some allergy medicine. I meet him in the downstairs bathroom, grab a towel from the closet, and hand it to him. He dries his feet off, and I join him on the edge of the tub.

"Can I see your foot?" I ask.

He gently lays it in my lap. I analyze his ankle and it's covered in swollen purple welts. They're huge and hard. I squeeze the cream out and rub it into the bites. He moans. When I finish one ankle, I do the other.

"It's really bad," I say, giving him his prognosis. "You gotta stop scratching."

"But it feels so good."

"It's the forbidden scratch. The more you do it, the worse it gets."

We head back to the kitchen, and I grab a water bottle for the allergy medicine and fill a plastic bag with ice from the fridge's ice maker. At the kitchen table, I pull out a chair for him to put his feet on and lay the ice bag, wrapped in a towel, on his swollen bites. "Give it a few minutes, and you should be all better."

I hand the allergy medicine and water bottle to him. He lays them on the table then reaches out for me instead. I scurry into his arms. "You're good at this." His palm is spread wide on my lower back.

I grasp his face, lean down for a kiss, and smile. He pulls me closer to kiss me deeper. A door slams shut outside. Peeking out the blinds, I groan. Mom's home. It's like she senses when I'm having a good time.

"Mom's here," I say untangling myself from his arms and standing a few feet away from him. When Mom walks past the kitchen blinds and sees Kamron, her eyes widen and turns back towards me. I bury my head, knowing she's about to yell at me.

"Kamron!" she says when she opens the door. Markese trails

behind her. "Naima didn't tell me you were coming over to-day."

"Yeah, I had some pretty bad mosquito bites and she offered to help me out," he explains to her.

Mom looks down at his feet on the chair and the ice pack on his ankles and back at me. "I see. Well you're welcome to stay and have dinner with us if you'd like." She shares her hostess smile.

He smiles back. "I would. Thank you." When his gaze turns to me, my cheeks burn.

"Naima, can I talk to you?" Mom points her head towards her room. Kamron asks Markese what game he's playing, and I follow Mom to her room. She shuts the door. "A few ground rules: no boys in the house when I'm not here. Look, I'm okay with you having a boyfriend—."

"He's not my boyfriend," I clarify. I know we kissed and said we liked each other, but he never asked me to be his girlfriend so I guess that means he's not my boyfriend.

Mom holds her breath, squints her eyes, and sits on the edge of her bed.

"Okay," she says slowly, "Well I'm fine with you dating, just don't have boys here when I'm not here. No dates on school nights and be home around eleven on the weekend."

"Eleven?" I wrinkle my nose. "That's past my bedtime."

"Of course." Mom shakes her head. "Surprisingly, I think you're the child I need to worry about the least." She crosses her arms and leans back on the bed. "So...do you like him?"

"Mom!" I roll my head back, embarrassed. Can she not ask me questions like this?

"You do." She smiles. "Do you need to go on birth control? Do you remember how to use a condom?"

"Mom!" I exhale deeply. "No and yes."

When my period first started, Mom—being the science teacher she is—showed me how the entire reproductive system worked, how birth control worked, and how to use condoms correctly. She figured that the more I knew, the less curious I'd be about having sex. She was right. I wanted very little to do with sex after watching *The Miracle of Life* and seeing a live birth.

"Okay." She studies me.

"So you're saying you're okay? With me having a boyfriend?"

"When I was your age—" She smiles from the memory then shifts on the bed. "You're a lot better than me, let's just say that. It does help that Kamron's a sweet boy. I told you he likes you."

I smile. "You did."

"I be knowin." She waves me out of her room before yelling, "Use protection! God knows you can't get an abortion in this state."

"Mom!" I turn back to her. I hope Kamron didn't hear that. When I walk back into the kitchen, Kamron's hiding his grin.

He definitely heard her.

"She said she's okay with me dating, but you can't be here when she's not."

He puts his hands up. "I get it." His lips slowly turn upwards into a grin. "So you're saying we're dating?"

I rub my thumb and inch my way towards him. "Um...I'm saying we went on a date so I mean, technically, that means dating."

"Hmm. I think dating means more than one date. So I'd have to take you out. Again." He smiles, reaching his hand out for mine.

I interlock my fingers with his. "Are you asking me out?"

"Only if you're accepting. And I promise, you won't need protection."

He laughs, and I swat at him as he pulls me closer into a hug.

Chapter Twenty-Four

Our second date is at his house four days after he asked. Kamron says he wants to show me something so I join him after school. He lives near the square—less than five minutes from the school. It's raining so when he parks in the driveway, he holds his raincoat over his head and walks over to the passenger side. My hair is already in need of a good wash so I don't mind walking in the rain, but he insists.

He opens the door so I can get out and canopies his jacket over my hair and body. We walk, our legs bumping, as we head to the door.

"You good?" he asks once we're under the awning.

I nod, and he fumbles through his keys for his house key. When he opens the door, it opens to a sunken living room and a bedroom straight ahead. On my left is the kitchen. He puts the keys on a side table that has a vase with blues, greens, and reds swirled into it. I'm about to reach out and touch it when Kamron grabs my hands.

"What I wanted to show you is back here." He leads me

down the hallway to my right. He throws his book bag into the room on one side, and on the other, he turns on the lights. The grayness outside makes the room extra bright so I turn the light off.

"Sorry," he says.

"It's okay."

I follow him into the room. Tables line one wall with clay, tools, and brushes. There are projects in various stages and near the back wall are his more finished projects. I lift one of the pieces in my hands. It's a sculpture that's wider on the bottom with a small ball on top. Like the vase near the front, yellows, reds, and blues are swirled into this one, and I run my fingers across its smooth glazed surface. On the other wall, he has a floor to ceiling bookshelf with multiple books on art and pottery in the middle but at the top there's books by authors like Toni Morrison, Jesmyn Ward, and Akwaeke Emezi, and on the bottom are ones by James Baldwin, Ta-Nehisi Coates, and Kiese Laymon. It's kinda impressive that he reads without being forced to.

I continue to make my way around the room. In the center is his pottery wheel sitting on top of a thick sheet, and a stool behind the wheel. I sit in the stool and press the pedal, pretending to shape clay.

"I can show you how to make something if you want," Kamron says. He's standing by the doorway, leaning up against the wall with his hands behind his back. He's been watching me this entire time.

"I'd love that." I smile.

As he walks towards me, I finish scanning his room. In the corner near the door, he has a nook setup. A teal armchair with a small round side table in front of it. On top of a table is a blue gift box. I point at it.

"Is that for me?" I grin.

"Yeah." He stops mid step and pivots back to the box. He carefully lifts it and hands it to me. It has weight to it. I shake it to see if I can guess what it is, but as I do, he presses his hands over mine. "Please don't shake it."

A tinge of hurt strikes my chest from his slight reprimand. I breathe deeply to release it and lift the cover off the box. Inside are a teapot and mug. I take the teapot out first and inspect it. It's a mix of greens and browns. I open the little cap on it and rub my fingers inside its smooth surface. I put the teapot down and pick up the mug. It's a tapered mug, where the bottom is slimmer than the top. It's the same blend of green and brown, and it feels sturdy in my hands. I can't believe he made this with his hands.

"You made this for me?" I ask.

"Yeah," he slides a stool from the table to the other side of the pottery wheel. "I used green because you wear a lot of green and when I met you, your hair was green and also Mississippi is really green."

My fingers glide across the glazed surface of the mug. I'm

guessing the brown is for my skin. During quarantine when I asked him about the teapot, he said he was feeling inspired. Inspired by me.

"This is the sweetest thing anyone has ever done for me." Tears build in my throat, and I don't try to mask it. I want him to know how touched I am.

He reaches his hand across the wheel. I set the mug back in the box and grab his hand. He tugs it slightly so I get up and sit in his lap. His arms wrap around my waist and mine around his neck. Gazing at him, I remember this boy who I swore had it out for me, who I'd rather be partners with anyone else but him. This boy who—when he found out about my autism—accepted and supported me. This boy who made me feel comfortable talking about my dad again. Who made me feel seen. This boy with the pretty eyelashes and perfect smile.

The rain continues to pitter pat against the window. I rub my thumb against his prickly scalp. My palm finds its way to his nape, and I admire him. This beautiful wonderful boy who I'm lucky to share this time and space with.

He wipes a tear from my cheek that I didn't even realize had fallen.

"Can I ask you a question?" he whispers, the words so close to me that I can taste them.

"Yeah."

He gulps, "Naima Grace Jones, will you be my girlfriend?"

He used my whole name. My heart's squealing right now,

but I exhale and attempt to play it cool.

"How did you know my middle name, creeper?"

"Naima Grace is your name on social media."

It's true.

"What's your middle name then?" I ask.

It's Alexander. I found it in my research on him months ago, but I never found a good time to bring it up organically.

"Alexander."

I playfully press a finger into his shoulder. "I will be your girlfriend, only if you Kamron Alexander Barksdale will be my boyfriend."

He tightens his grip around my waist, grins, and says, "Bet."

Let's see what the stars have in store for us.

Acknowledgements

This book is sixteen years in the making, and I'm so glad it's now in your hands. It's everything I ever dreamed of and more, and I hope it leaves you with some heartwarming wisdom.

First, I want to thank me. I always make a habit of thanking everybody while dismissing the role I played in it. This book would not have been possible if I did not sit down and commit to telling this story. I showed up over the course of two years and wrote, edited, revised, formatted, designed, and published this book. *About the Boy* is here because of my dedication, consistency, and work.

As always, thank you to my ancestors for your love, support, and guidance during this publishing journey. This book would've been a distant memory if not for the series of events that led to me remembering, sitting down, and writing it. Speaking of which, a special thank you to Tracy Deonn for *Legendborn*. It was that book specifically that triggered this story in me and reminded me of the possibilities of young adult literature. I'm forever grateful for what you've offered to the world and am eagerly awaiting the next book.

Thank you Clydette deGroot and The deGroot Foundation for the Courage to Write Grant. When I received this grant, it allowed me the time I needed to finally make this lifelong dream a reality. That time was an invaluable gift. Thank you for seeing the work I was doing and financially supporting it.

Thank you Voyage YA for selecting an excerpt of *About the Boy* as a winner for the 2023 Novel Excerpt Contest. I'm honored that y'all saw the beauty and charm in Kamron and Naima's romance story and wanted to share it.

Thank you to the women behind Little Mix: Perrie Edwards, Leigh-Anne Pinnock, Jade Amelia Thirlwall and yes, even you Jesy Nelson. Your music has been a celebration, a balm, and a support throughout my late teens and twenties. We have grown up together, and y'all always bring the exact vibe I need for each season of my life. Even though I didn't intend for Little Mix to be featured so heavily, I wrote this when the group disbanded and I played your music nonstop. If anything, Little Mix made this book that much better.

Thank you Markese and Myiahnna for keeping me young and helping me with the tiny details of this story. Now I've named characters after the both of you!

Thank you Gunnar Boleen, Colton Moon, and Kenneth Nguyen for being nerds. Kidding! I really appreciate y'all's help shaping Kamron and Sam's special interests.

To Tianna Arrendondo, Adrienne Balton, Danielle Buckingham, Krystal Clarke, Mary Maeve George, Amanda Helander, Sally Howe, Petra Lurch and Nina Winters, thank you for your help with my shelved memoir. I appreciate the time and energy that y'all dedicated to that project even if it's not out in the world. Thank you for your constructive feedback and general support. Even though that project may never be published, it was the impetus that allowed *About the Boy* to exist.

As always thank you to my Creative Council: Catherine Arjet, Akanksha Aurora, Danielle (again!), Allie Judge, Rachel Long, Jenna Mayzouni, Ghrey Mbenza, Keely Parker, Bijal Patel, Nancey B. Price, and Amaris Ramey. Y'all have heard me ramble about this book for the better part of two years, and it's finally here. Thank you for your behind-the-scenes support and affirmations as I continue to work on writing and publishing these books. Our midnight stargazing in college showed me what romance between friends could look like and helped inspire Naima and Kamron's date scene. Your friendship is unmatched, and I'm forever grateful.

And finally, thank you to all of the readers, book influencers, and culture workers who have reached out and help spread the word about all of my work. Every time I see your posts and receive your interview requests, I'm grateful that you spent what precious time you have on this earth reading my stories. That is the highest honor. Thank you.

About the Author

Leah Nicole Whitcomb is a community storyteller from Mississippi who writes about Black folks, love, and magic. She co-hosts the Hoodoo Plant Mamas podcast. Her writing has been featured in *Sistories, Samjoko Magazine* and the young adult anthology, *All the Ways a Heart Burns*. A Courage to Write Grant recipient, Leah's work has been supported by The deGroot Foundation, Voices of Our Nation Arts Foundation, The Bereket Writing Community, Women of Color Writers Podcast, and the Women's National Book Association. She is the author of the short story collection, *Apocalypse Still*, and the young adult romance, *About the Boy*.

Between Us

Book 2

Naima

Prom. The single most important day in a teenager's life or so they say. I always imagined spending this day getting ready with my best friend Luna. We'd wear matching dresses, and she'd put her makeup skills to use to make me look magical. Luna's here. She's working on my eye shadow now, but so is Dixie.

Dixie Davis is my other best friend Sam's girlfriend. They're both TikTok creators although it seems like Dixie is siphoning Sam's followers. There's nothing particularly bad about her. She's a pretty girl, long brown hair, thin—it sounds like I'm describing a horse. She's not bad, really. I just, I don't know. She's trying to tell us about some beef she has with another creator that I don't care about, and I'm trying to be nice.

Say my "um hmms" and "yeah" at the right time, but this is supposed to be exciting. I'm supposed to be getting ready to dance the night away with Luna and enjoy our Saturday night, but instead we have to babysit Dixie.

"She's totally copying my style. I started the Y2K trend then she hopped on. I thought about dying my hair platinum blonde, and she went ahead and did it." Dixie spreads herself out on my bed. For someone who cares about her looks, she doesn't care that she's wrinkling her dress. "It's like I can't win."

"It's like I don't care," I mumble to Luna who snickers.

"Hold still, I'm almost done," Luna says, then looks at Dixie. "Girl, have you tried calling her out?"

Dixie springs up from the bed. "That's it! Everyone will know what a snake she is. Oh my god, Luna. You're the best."

"I know," Luna says while she finishes blending my smoky eye. When she's done, she moves out of the way for me to see myself in the mirror. I usually stray away from heavy eye makeup (because I don't know how to do it myself), but Luna is the best, and my brown eyes really pop. The rest of my makeup too, but I can't stop looking at my eyes and eyebrows. When she does my eyebrows, they look like twins. When I do them, they look like strangers.

"Luna" —I grab her hands— "I look amazing. How are you so great at everything?"

"I'm just naturally talented."

"You are!" I squeeze her and refuse to let go.

In two months, Luna is moving back to Mexico with her family, and I'll never see her again. Okay, maybe that's being dramatic. I will see her again. I can always video call her, but she won't be a fifteen minute drive away. We won't be able to spend the night at each other's house without a long flight. She can't help me get ready for major life events and do my makeup and make me look pretty.

"You can let go now," Luna says, straining from the pressure of my hug.

"I'm sorry. Who knows how long I'll get to hug you and—" My eyes start to water. Luna has been my best friend since the fifth grade when she moved here, and now she's leaving eight years later. Sure, I may have Sam—who's undecided about moving to Los Angeles with Dixie, and my boyfriend Kamron who decided to take a gap year, but Luna is everything. She's my everything.

Luna grabs a tissue and dots my eyes. "You better not mess up my makeup, girl. Two months is plenty of time. You have plenty of time with me."

I nod and swallow the tears building up in my throat. I have plenty of time left with Luna. Two months seem like so little, but we can make it plenty.

Luna unzips her garment bag and slides into her gown. I grab my dress from my closet and step into it, pulling it up over my body. Usually, we coordinate our outfits, but I saw the perfect dress over the summer and bought it without knowing the theme for prom. The theme is Old Hollywood and Luna used Megan Thee Stallion's Old Hollywood Met Gala look for inspiration. She's wearing a red sequin gown and has jumbo rollers in her hair. I saw this perfect teal and mint ombre tulle gown that I had to get so instead of matching with my best friend, I'm coordinating with my boyfriend. Where is he, by the way?

I grab my phone. He texted that he was on his way eleven minutes ago, so he should be here at any moment. I'm dressed. My makeup is done. My hair is a wash and go with a side part. I grab my gloves and shoes, and now I'm ready for prom.

Car doors slam outside so I look out the window and see Sam's burgundy Jeep, Kamron's white Prius, and Marcus's yellow Camaro. Kamron is leaning against his car in his black suit, and he looks so pretty with his hair braided like that. I smile remembering my first thoughts of him: pretty but annoying. A little too much of a golden boy, but I was definitely projecting. He's smart, thoughtful, patient, and yes very pretty. I can't believe he's mine.

"Our dates are here!" I yell even though the girls are right beside me.

"Darius is gonna get on my nerves," Luna groans. "I don't know why I agreed to go with him."

"You could've been my date," I remind her.

"And what about your boyfriend? I don't want to be a third

Luna hands Naima her phone back, and she swipes through the photos faster than I can even process it. Eventually, she shows me one and says, "How are you so cute? You look so much better than me."

My suit's a statement piece—black with mint and teal florals that match Naima's mint and teal dress. My aunt Amaya braided my hair into this cornrow design that feeds into a bun, and she trimmed my sides. My shoes are velvet tuxedos. I clean up okay.

The girls have already picked a table near the back wall, and I follow Naima there to sit. After about ten minutes, the rest of the group joins us right as the servers bring salad and drinks. Everyone's quietly pecking at their salad until Darius asks, "What y'all doing after this?"

"Mom told me to stay out til midnight so." Naima shrugs then looks over at me.

"I want to party if y'all wanna," Luna says, then mimes a joint with her fingers.

"We gotta wait til baseball season is over," Sam says.

"*He* gotta wait. I got you, baby girl." Darius winks at Luna, and she rolls her eyes. "You want in?" Darius asks me.

"Nah, man. I gotta take Naima home."

"Nigga, just spend the night. We staying at Sam's."

I mean I probably could spend the night. Amaya wouldn't mind, and I don't even remember the last time I got high. I sigh then look at Naima. I gotta be responsible, though. This is prom, and I want her to have a good time, too.

"I'm good."

Darius shakes his head like he doesn't believe me. I half believe me too, but Sam changes the subject.

"So y'all coming to our last game? Next Thursday?"

"Yes, of course." Naima wrinkles her nose. "You know how much I love baseball."

She hates all sports which she reminds me of every time I try to watch a NBA or NFL game with her.

"It's against Cherokee Central. We're gonna whoop their ass," Marcus chimes in.

"Haven't y'all lost most of your games this year?" Naima asks in her gentle tone with the straightest face that makes it ten times funnier.

As I snort, Sam responds, "That's not important. We just gotta finish strong."

The guys high five each other and repeat, "Finish strong."

The rest of the food comes, and we eat. As soon as the music starts, Naima grabs Luna's hand and runs to the dance floor. While everyone else cares how they dance, and if it's cool enough, Naima doesn't. She moves in whatever way she feels called which makes it more admirable. I grab my phone and record a few clips of her that I know she'll appreciate later and then I sit back in my chair and open my email.

It's been a habit I've had almost every day for the past month. While Naima was applying to college, I sent my portfolio to galleries across the country and a few international ones as well. The deadline for a few of them passed a couple of months ago so I'm just waiting for an acceptance. So far, I've gotten one rejection, but there are still a dozen other places I'm waiting to hear from. The problem is I haven't told Naima any of this. She thinks I'm taking a gap year, and that's partially true. I'm not planning on going to college next year...or any year after that. The truth of that may devastate her as well as the truth of—

Naima grabs my shoulder, jolting me out of my thoughts. She's holding her hand out to me while the music slows down. I grab her hand and follow her to the dance floor. Laying her sweaty head on my shoulder, she presses her body into mine and sways. Damn, even her sweat smells good. I close my eyes, following along to her body and the music. Something hard and sharp slides between us and when I open my eyes, Mrs. Berry, our precalculus teacher, is there with a yardstick in her hand.

"Y'all need to keep Jesus between you," she says and presses the stick into my belly. I back away from Naima who I catch rolling her eyes.

"I'm sorry, Mrs. Berry," I say and smile knowing it'll diffuse the scowl on her face. It does, and she walks away. I cup Naima's jaw. She leans into it and hums. "Sorry about that," I say and bring her hand to my lips to kiss her knuckles. Softly. Apologetically.

"It's whatever." She tries to play it off but yawns. The fatigue is setting in the corners of her face.

"You wanna sit down?" I ask.

"It's prom!" She releases herself from me and throws her hands in the air. "We're supposed to have fun."

"But we can take a break." I hold my hand out to give her the choice of taking it. Begrudgingly she does so I lead her back to our seats. Her shoulder slumps, and her face softens when she looks back at the dance floor, at our friends dancing, talking, and laughing with each other.

"We can go home," I remind her. She has options other than exhausting herself to keep up with everybody else.

She rubs her eyes and then looks at me. "No, I'm fine. We can stay a bit longer." Naima squeezes my hand and offers a tired smile. She looks longingly at the dance floor for a few more songs until a pop song comes on. She instantly brightens and grabs me. "You have to dance with me."

I try to follow along with her dance moves. She twists and turns then punches the air and punches the dance floor. At one point she backs up on me and grinds, stopping when the chorus returns. Then, she jumps some more until the music finishes.

"Okay, I'm ready to go," she pants. "Let me go tell Luna."

Naima taps Luna's shoulder while she's dancing with some guy who's not her date.

"You're leaving? Noooo," Luna whines then hugs Naima.

They squeeze each other for a good solid minute. "Ask your mom if I can spend the night. I'm not sleeping on Sam's couch."

"Okay, I will," Naima says. She looks around for Sam and then waves goodbye to him before we leave.

In the car, I ask her if she wants to get ice cream or something before I take her home. It's only 9:26.

"I just feel bad. This is your prom, and I'm making you leave early."

"You didn't make me do anything I didn't want to do," I reassure her.

Out of my peripheral, she stares at me then twists her lips. She's uncertain. I grab her hand and rub my thumb over her knuckles. "You don't have to go home yet. We can go somewhere else."

Her face brightens then. "Okay. Yes."

We drive to the nearest park and sit under the trees. Cracking the windows, I turn off the car, take off my suit jacket, get out of the driver's seat and into the backseat. Naima climbs over the seats to get into the back. She rests her head in my lap, and I rub her shoulders.

"Did you have fun at least?" I ask. The park light adds a soft warm light to the car, and the cicadas hum in the humid night air.

She sighs, "Why do people make such a big deal out of prom? It's a lot of pressure to have a great time and to go all out. I mean it was fun, but it was no different than any other school dance."

"It's the last time we all get together and party before we graduate. That's a pretty big deal."

"I don't know. I guess the way people talked about it. I thought I'd feel differently."

"Yeah, I get that." Prom is more of an ideal than anything else. We think it's a bigger deal than it is because we've made it that way.

But I change the subject. Something I've learned that she likes is when I indulge her in her special interests and theories. It's always a fun thought experiment, and it's exciting to see where we end up.

"What's the latest theory?"

She hums, thinking about the question and then asks, "Are aliens racist?"

I choke-laugh. Where does she come up with this? "Why do you say that?"

"I was watching a documentary about alien abductions and all the interviewees were white so either aliens are racist and only want white people or people of color don't talk about their alien abductions, but if aliens only want white people why? Are aliens racist and hate the rest of us? Are they experimenting on white people? If so, why?"

That was a lot, but I ask, "Do you want to be abducted by aliens?"

"No!" she answers quickly. "That sounds terrifying. I just don't like the idea of aliens preferring white people. Like is white supremacy intergalactic?"

"I think if a species is advanced enough for intergalactic travel, I don't think they care about racial politics. Maybe Black folks just don't talk about alien abductions cause they'll probably lock us up."

"That could be it, but I don't know," she yawns. "It doesn't sit right with me that aliens are racist."

I rub her shoulder while she stammers through a sentence, "I just—it doesn't." After a few seconds she gives up and breathes softly. Her eyelids flutter shut, and she's out. I rub her arm a little bit longer. She looks so peaceful, and it's going to be my fault when she's not anymore. I sigh knowing that in one-hundred and five days, I'm going to break her heart.

Naima and Kamron's story continues in *Between Us*, the sequel to *About the Boy*.

9 7989899 36823